BLOOD MONEY

The Persons this *Mystery* is about—

PERCY MAGUIRE,
the Continental Detective Agency's operative (who assumes the name on the spur of the moment), is a short and lumpy man who is aware that it is not healthy in criminal circles to be seen wagging your chin with a sleuth right after a job has been turned.

JACK COUNIHAN,
a tall, slender lad of twenty-three or twenty-four, on his first job for Continental because he thought gumshoeing would be fun. He would rather catch the wrong man than wear the wrong necktie.

ANDREW MacELROY,
another operative for Continental—a big boulder of a man, glum and grim with no more imagination than an adding machine, and too dumb not to do what he was told.

BIG FLORA BRACE,
an underworld big shot—a broad-shouldered, thick-armed, deep-bosomed woman with a pink throat which, for all its smoothness, is muscled like a wrestler's. About forty, with very curly and very yellow bobbed hair, and a handsome, brutal face; she is no toy.

PAPADOPOULOS,
a shabby little old man with scary brown eyes, a straggly yellow-white mustache, and the movements of a rheumatic rabbit, who pleads that he is too old and sick for prison.

BLUEPOINT VANCE,
a sharp-eyed, sharp-nosed criminal, with lips thin as knife edges under a small painted mustache—shrewd and resourceful with a weakness common to his type.

TOM-TOM CAREY,
whose real name was Alfredo Estanislao Cristobal Carrera—a tall, thick-chested, thin-bellied 190-pounder with a swarthy face and a hard fist, who had been captured variously, but never convicted.

RED O'LEARY,
a wide-shouldered young giant with fiery red hair, blue eyes, and a ruddy face that is good looking in a tough, savage way.

ANN NEWHALL,
a millionaire's daughter who mistakes a glorious roughneck for a romantic figure and thinks a little crime is fun.

ANGEL GRACE CARDIGAN,
who is known to her pals as Nellie Wade—a thief among thieves, who was an accomplished grifter at nineteen.

BLOOD MONEY

Things this *Mystery* is about—

TWO WORDS written in blood on a gray wall . . .

A SPRING KNIFE with a long blade . . .

A .38 SPECIAL . . .

FILE 1361-C . . .

Green bundles of MONEY with yellow wrappers . . .

A REWARD of $106,000 . . .

An 18-inch length of LEAD PIPE stuffed in a garden hose

A limp brown BLACKJACK . . .

A *PRIVATE OPERATIVE* MURDER STORY

BLOOD MONEY

By DASHIELL HAMMETT

Author of "The Maltese Falcon," "The Thin Man," "Red Harvest," "The Glass Key," etc.

DELL PUBLISHING COMPANY

George T. Delacorte, Jr., *President* • Helen Meyer, *Vice-President*

149 Madison Avenue *Printed in U.S.A.* New York 16, N. Y.

BLOOD MONEY

List of *Exciting* Chapters—

Part I: THE BIG WOMAN

Part II: THE LITTLE OLD MAN

Part One

THE BIG WOMAN

Blood Money

Chapter One

WHAT'S THE CAPER?

I FOUND Paddy the Mex in Jean Larrouy's dive.

Paddy—an amiable con man who looked like the King of Spain—showed me his big white teeth in a smile, pushed a chair out for me with one foot, and told the girl who shared his table:

"Nellie, meet the biggest-hearted dick in San Francisco. This little fat guy will do anything for anybody, if only he can send 'em over for life in the end." He turned to me, waving his cigar at the girl: "Nellie Wade, and you can't get anything on her. She don't have to work—her old man's a bootlegger."

She was a slim girl in blue—white skin, long green eyes, short chestnut hair. Her sullen face livened into beauty when she put a hand across the table to me, and we both laughed at Paddy.

"Five years?" she asked.

"Six," I corrected.

"Damn!" said Paddy, grinning and hailing a waiter. "Some day I'm going to fool a sleuth."

So far he had fooled all of them—he had never slept in a hoosegow.

I looked at the girl again. Six years before, this Angel Grace Cardigan had buncoed half a dozen Philadelphia boys out of plenty. Dan Morey and I had nailed her, but none of her victims would go to bat against her, so she had been turned loose. She was a kid of nineteen then, but already a smooth grifter.

In the middle of the floor one of Larrouy's girls began to sing *Tell Me What You Want and I'll Tell You What You Get*. Paddy the Mex tipped a gin-bottle over the glasses of ginger ale the waiter had brought. We drank and I gave Paddy a piece of paper with a name and address penciled on it.

"Itchy Maker asked me to slip you that," I explained. "I saw him in the Folsom big house yesterday. It's his mother he says, and he wants you to look her up and see if she wants anything. What he means, I suppose, is that you're to give her his cut from the last trick you and he turned."

"You hurt my feelings," Paddy said, pocketing the paper and bringing out the gin again.

I downed the second gin-ginger ale and gathered in my feet, preparing to rise and trot along home.

At that moment four of Larrouy's clients came in from the street. Recognition of one of them kept me in my chair. He was tall, slender and all dolled up in what the well-dressed man should wear. Sharp-eyed, sharp-faced, with lips thin as knife-edges under a small pointed mustache—Bluepoint Vance. I wondered what he was doing three thousand miles away from his New York hunting-grounds.

While I wondered I put the back of my head to him, pretending interest in the singer, who was now giving the customers *I Want to Be a Bum*. Beyond her, back in a corner, I spotted another familiar face that belonged in another city—Happy Jim Hacker, round and rosy Detroit gunman twice sentenced to death and twice pardoned.

When I faced front again, Bluepoint Vance and his three companions had come to rest two tables away. His back was to us. I sized up his playmates.

Facing Vance sat a wide-shouldered young giant with red hair, blue eyes and a ruddy face that was good-looking in a tough, savage way. On his left was a shifty-eyed dark girl in a floppy hat. She was talking to Vance. The red-haired giant's attention was all taken by the fourth member of the party, on his right. She deserved it.

She was neither tall nor short, thin nor plump. She

wore a black Russian tunic affair, green-trimmed and hung with silver dinguses. A black fur coat was spread over the chair behind her. She was probably twenty. Her eyes were blue, her mouth red, her teeth white, the hair-ends showing under her black-green-and-silver turban were brown, and she had a nose. Without getting steamed up over the details, she was nice. I said so. Paddy the Mex agreed with a "That's what," and Angel Grace suggested that I go over and tell Red O'Leary I thought her nice.

"Red O'Leary the big bird?" I asked, sliding down in my seat so I could stretch a foot under the table between Paddy and Angel Grace. "Who's his nice girl friend?"

"Nancy Regan, and the other one's Sylvia Yount.'

"And the slicker with his back to us?" I probed.

Paddy's foot, hunting the girl's under the table, bumped mine.

"Don't kick me, Paddy," I pleaded. "I'll be good. Anyway, I'm not going to stay here to be bruised. I'm going home."

I swapped so-longs with them and moved toward the street, keeping my back to Bluepoint Vance.

At the door I had to step aside to let two men come in. Both knew me, but neither gave me a tumble—Sheeny Holmes (not the old-timer who staged the Moose Jaw looting back in the buggy-riding days) and Denny Burke, Baltimore's King of Frog Island. A good pair—neither of them would think of taking a life unless assured of profit and political protection.

Outside, I turned down toward Kearny Street, strolling along, thinking that Larrouy's joint had been full of crooks this one night, and that there seemed to be more than a sprinkling of prominent visitors in our midst.

A shadow in a doorway interrupted my brainwork.

The shadow said, "Ps-s-s-s!"

Stopping, I examined the shadow until I saw it was Beno, a hophead newsie who had given me a tip now and then in the past—some good, some phony.

"I'm sleepy," I growled as I joined Beno and his armload of newspapers in the doorway, "and I've heard the story about the Mormon who stuttered, so if that's what's on your mind, say so, and I'll keep going."

"I don't know nothin' about no Mormons," he protested, "but I know somethin' else."

"Well?"

" 'S all right for you to say 'Well,' but what I want to know is, what am I gonna get out of it?"

"Flop in the nice doorway and go shut-eye," I advised him, moving toward the street again. "You'll be all right when you wake up."

"Hey! Listen I got somethin' for you. Hones' to

Gawd!"

"Well?"

"Listen!" He came close, whispering. "There's a caper rigged for the Seaman's National. I don't know what's the racket, but it's real. . . . Hones' to Gawd! I ain't stringin' you. I can't give you no monickers. You know I would if I knowed 'em. Hones' to Gawd. Gimme ten bucks. It's worth that to you, ain't it? This is straight dope—hones' to Gawd!"

"Yeah, straight from the nose-candy!"

"No! Hones' to Gawd! I—"

"What *is* the caper, then?"

"I don't know. All I got was that the Seaman's is gonna be nicked. Hones' to—"

"Where'd you get it?"

Beno shook his head. I put a silver dollar in his hand.

"Get another shot and think up the rest of it," I told him, "and if it's amusing enough I'll give you the other nine bucks."

I walked on down to the corner, screwing up my forehead over Beno's tale. By itself, it sounded like what it probably was—a yarn designed to get a dollar out of a trusting gumshoe. But it wasn't altogether by itself. Larrouy's—just one drum in a city that had a number —had been heavy with grifters who were threats against life and property. It was worth a look-see, especially since the insurance company covering the Seaman's National Bank was a Continental Detective Agency client.

Around the corner, twenty feet or so along Kearny Street, I stopped.

From the street I had just quit came two bangs—the reports of a heavy pistol.

I went back the way I had come. As I rounded the corner I saw men gathering in a group up the street. A young Armenian—a dapper boy of nineteen or twenty—passed me, going the other way, sauntering along, hands in pockets, softly whistling *Broken-hearted Sue.*

I joined the group—now becoming a crowd—around Beno. Beno was dead, blood from two holes in his chest staining the crumpled newspapers under him.

I went up to Larrouy's and looked in. Red O'Leary, Bluepoint Vance, Nancy Regan, Sylvia Yount, Paddy the Mex, Angel Grace, Denny Burke, Sheeny Holmes, Happy Jim Hacker—not one of them was there.

Returning to Beno's vicinity, I loitered with my back to a wall while the police arrived, asked questions, learned nothing, found no witnesses, and departed, taking what was left of the newsie with them

I went home and to bed.

Chapter Two

Hell on a Holiday

In the morning I spent one hour in the Agency file-room, digging through the gallery and records. We didn't have anything on Red O'Leary, Denny Burke, Nancy Regan, Sylvia Yount, and only some guesses on Paddy the Mex. Nor were there any open jobs definitely chalked against Angel Grace, Bluepoint Vance, Sheeny Holmes and Happy Jim Hacker, but their photos were there.

At ten o'clock—bank opening time—I set out for the Seaman's National, carrying these photos and Beno's tip.

The Continental Detective Agency's San Francisco office is located in a Market Street office building. The Seaman's National Bank occupies the ground floor of a tall gray building in Montgomery Street, San Francisco's financial center. Ordinarily, since I don't like even seven blocks of unnecessary walking, I would have taken a street car. But there was some sort of traffic jam on Market Street, so I set out afoot, turning off along

Grand Avenue.

A few blocks of walking, and I began to see that something was wrong with the part of town I was heading for. Noises for one thing—roaring, rattling, explosive noises.

At Sutter Street a man passed me, holding his face with both hands and groaning as he tried to push a dislocated jaw back in place. His cheek was scraped red.

I went down Sutter Street. Traffic was in a tangle that reached to Montgomery Street. Excited, bare-headed men were running around. The explosive noises were clearer. An automobile full of policemen went down past me, going as fast as traffic would let it. An ambulance came up the street, clanging its gong, taking to the sidewalks where traffic was worst.

I crossed Kearny Street on the trot. Down the other side of the street two patrolmen were running. One had his gun out. The explosive noises were a drumming chorus ahead.

Rounding into Montgomery Street, I found few sightseers ahead of me. The middle of the street was filled with trucks, touring cars, taxis—deserted there. Up in the next block—between Bush and Pine Streets—hell was on a holiday.

The holiday spirit was gayest in the middle of the block, where the Seaman's National Bank and the

Golden Gate Trust Company faced each other across the street.

For the next six hours I was busier than a flea on a fat woman.

Chapter Three

The Old Man

Late that afternoon I took a recess from bloodhounding and went up to the office for a pow-wow with the Old Man. He was leaning back in his chair, staring out the window, tapping on his desk with the customary long yellow pencil.

A tall, plump man in his seventies, this boss of mine, with a white-mustached, baby-pink, grandfatherly face, mild blue eyes behind rimless spectacles, and no more warmth in him than a hangman's rope. Fifty years of crook-hunting for the Continental had emptied him of everything except brains and a soft-spoken, gently smiling shell politeness that was the same whether things went good or bad—and means as little at one time as another. We who worked under him were proud of his cold-bloodedness. We used to boast that he could spit icicles in July, and we called him Pontius Pilate among ourselves, because he smiled politely when he sent us out to be crucified on suicidal jobs.

He turned from the window as I came in, nodded me

to a chair, and smoothed his mustache with the pencil. On his desk the afternoon papers screamed the news of the Seaman's National Bank and Golden Gate Trust Company double-looting in five colors.

"What is the situation?" he asked, as one would ask about the weather.

"The situation is a pip," I told him. "There were a hundred and fifty crooks in the push if there was one. I saw a hundred myself, or think I did—and there were slews of them that I didn't see—planted where they could jump out and bite when fresh teeth were needed. They bit, too. They bushwacked the police and made a merry wreck out of 'em—going and coming. They hit the two banks at ten sharp—took over the whole block—chased away the reasonable people—dropped the others. The actual looting was duck soup to a mob of that size. Twenty or thirty of 'em to each of the banks while the others held the street. Nothing to it but wrap up the spoils and take 'em home.

"There's a highly indignant businessmen's meeting down there now—wild-eyed stockholders up on their hind legs yelling for the chief of police's heart's blood. The police didn't do any miracles, that's a cinch, but no police department is equipped to handle a trick of that size—no matter how well they think they are. The whole thing lasted less than twenty minutes. There were, say, a hundred and fifty thugs in on it, loaded for bear, every play mapped to the inch. How are you going to get enough coppers down there, size up the racket, plan your battle, and put it over in that little time? It's easy enough to say the police should look ahead—should have a dose for every emergency—but these same birds who are yelling, 'Rotten,' down there now would be the first to squawk, 'Robbery,' if their taxes were boosted a couple of cents to buy more policemen and equipment.

"But the police fell down—there's no question about that—and there will be a lot of beefy necks feel the ax. The armored cars were no good, the grenading was about fifty-fifty, since the bandits knew how to play that game, too. But the real disgrace of the party was the police machine guns. The bankers and brokers are saying they were fixed. Whether they were deliberately tampered with, or were only carelessly taken care of, is anybody's guess, but only one of the damned things would shoot, and it not very well.

"The getaway was north on Montgomery to Columbus. Along Columbus the parade melted, a few cars at a time, into side streets. The police ran into an ambush between Washington and Jackson, and by the time they had shot their way through it the bandit cars had scattered all over the city. A lot of 'em have been picked up since then—empty.

"All the returns aren't in yet, but right now the score stands something like this:

"The haul will run God only knows how far into the millions—easily the richest pickings ever got with civilian guns. Sixteen coppers were knocked off, and three times that many wounded. Twelve innocent spectators, bank clerks, and the like, were killed and about as many banged around. There are two bandits and five shot-ups who might be either thugs or spectators that got too close. The bandits lost seven dead that we know of and thirty-one prisoners, most of them bleeding somewhere.

"One of the dead was Fat Boy Clarke. Remember him? He shot his way out of a Des Moines courtroom three or four years ago. Well, in his pocket we found a piece of paper, a map of Montgomery Street between Pine and Bush, the block of the looting. On the back of the map were typed instructions, telling him exactly what to do and when to do it. An X on the map showed him where he was to park the car in which he arrived with his seven men, and there was a circle where he was to stand with them, keeping an eye on things in general and on the windows and roofs of the buildings across the street in particular. Figures 1, 2, 3, 4, 5, 6, 7, 8 on the map marked doorways, steps, a deep window, and so on, that were to be used for shelter if shots had to be traded with those windows and roofs. Clarke was to pay no attention to the Bush Street end of the block, but if the police charged the Pine Street end he was to move his men up there, distributing them among points marked a, b, c, d, e, f, g, and h. (His body was found on the spot marked a.)

"Every five minutes during the looting he was to send a man to an automobile standing in the street at a point marked on the map with a star, to see if there were any new instructions. He was to tell his men that if he were shot down one of them must report to the car, and a new leader would be given them. When the signal for the getaway was given, he was to send one of his men to the car in which he had come. If it was still in commission, this man was to drive it, not passing the car ahead of him. If it was out of whack, the man was to report to the star-marked car for instructions how to get a new one. I suppose they counted on finding enough parked cars to take care of this end. While Clarke waited for his car he and his men were to throw as much lead as possible at every target in their district, and none of them was to board the car until it came abreast of them. Then they were to drive out Montgomery to Columbus to—blank.

"Get that?" I asked. "Here are a hundred and fifty gunmen, split into groups under group-leaders, with maps and schedules showing what each man is to do, showing the fire-plug he's to kneel behind, the brick he's to stand on, where he's to spit—everything but the name and address of the policeman he's to shoot! It's just as well Beno couldn't give me the details—I'd have written it off as a hophead's dream!"

"Very interesting," the Old Man said, smiling blandly.

"The Fat Boy's was the only timetable we found," I went on with my history. "I saw a few friends among the killed and caught, and the police are still identifying others. Some are local talent, but most of 'em seem to be imported stock. Detroit, Chi, New York, St. Louis, Denver, Portland, L. A., Philly, Baltimore—all seem to have sent delegates. As soon as the police get through identifying them I'll make out a list.

"Of those who weren't caught, Bluepoint Vance seems to be the main squeeze. He was in the car that directed operations. I don't know who else was there with him. The Shivering Kid was in on the festivities, and I think Alphabet Shorty McCoy though I didn't get a good look at him. Sergeant Bender told me he spotted Toots Salda and Darby M'Laughlin in the push, and Morgan saw the Dis-and-Dat Kid. That's a good cross-section of the layout—gunmen, swindlers, hijackers from all over Rand-McNally.

"The Hall of Justice has been a slaughter-house all

afternoon. The police haven't killed any of their guests—none that I know of—but they're sure-God making believers out of them. Newspaper writers who like to sob over what they call the third degree should be down there now. After being knocked around a bit, some of the guests have talked. But the hell of it is they don't know a whole lot. They know some names—Denny Burke, Toby the Lugs, Old Pete Best, Fat Boy Clarke and Paddy the Mex were named—and that helps some, but all the smacking power in the police force arm can't bring out anything else.

"The racket seems to have been organized like this:

"Denny Burke, for instance, is known as a shifty worker in Baltimore. Well, Denny talks to eight or ten likely boys, one at a time. 'How'd you like to pick up a piece of change out on the Coast?' he asks them. 'Doing what?' the candidate wants to know. 'Doing what you're told,' the King of Frog Island says. 'You know me. I'm telling you this is the fastest picking ever rigged, a kick in the pants to go through—air-tight. Everybody in on it will come home lousy with cash—and they'll all come home if they don't dog it. That's all I'm spilling. If you don't like it—forget it.'

"And these birds did know Denny, and if he said the job was good that was enough for them. So they put in with him. He told them nothing. He saw that they had guns, gave 'em each a ticket to San Francisco and twenty bucks, and told them where to meet him here. Last night he collected them and told them they went to work this morning. By that time they had moved around the town enough to see that it was bubbling over with visiting talent, including such moguls as Toots Salda, Bluepoint Vance and the Shivering Kid. So this morning they went forth eagerly with the King of Frog Island at their head to do their stuff.

"The other talkers tell varieties of the same tale. The police found room in their crowded jail to stick in a few stool-pigeons. Since few of the bandits knew very many of the others, the stools had an easy time of it, but the only thing they could add to what we've got is that the prisoners are looking for a wholesale delivery to-night. They seem to think their mob will crash the prison and turn 'em loose. That's probably a lot of chewing-gum, but anyway this time the police will be ready.

"That's the situation as it stands now. The police are sweeping the streets, picking up everybody who needs a shave or can't show a certificate of attendance signed by his parson with special attention to outward bound trains, boats and automobiles. I sent Jack Counihan and Dick Foley down North Beach way to play the joints and see if they can pick up anything."

"Do you think Bluepoint Vance was the actual directing intelligence in this robbery?" the Old Man asked.

"I hope so—we know him."

The Old Man turned his chair so his mild eyes could stare out the window again, and he tapped his desk reflectively with the pencil.

"I'm afraid not," he said in a gently apologetic tone. "Vance is a shrewd, resourceful and determined criminal, but his weakness is one common to his type. His abilities are all for present action and not for planning ahead. He has executed some large operations, but I've always thought I saw in them some other mind at work behind him."

I couldn't quarrel with that. If the Old Man said something was so, then it probably was, because he was one of these cautious babies who'll look out of the window at a cloudburst and say, "It seems to be raining," on the off-chance that somebody's pouring water off the roof.

"And who is this arch-gonnif?" I asked.

"You'll probably know that before I do," he said, smiling benignantly.

Chapter Four

THE SKULL-CRACKER AND THE GOOSE

I WENT BACK to the Hall and helped boil more prisoners in oil until around eight o'clock, when my appetite reminded me I hadn't eaten since breakfast. I attended to that, and then turned down toward Larrouy's, ambling along leisurely, so the exercise wouldn't interfere with my digestion.

I spent three-quarters of an hour in Larrouy's, and didn't see anybody who interested me especially. A few gents I know were present, but they weren't anxious to associate with me—it's not always healthy in criminal circles to be seen wagging your chin with a sleuth right after a job has been turned.

Not getting anything there, I moved up the street to Wop Healy's—another hole. My reception was the same here—I was given a table and let alone. Healy's orchestra was giving *Don't You Cheat* all they had while those customers who felt athletic were roughing it out on the dance floor. One of the dancers was Jack Counihan, his arms full of a big olive-skinned girl with a pleasant, thick-featured stupid face.

Jack was a tall, slender lad of twenty-three or -four who had drifted into the Continental's employ a few months before. It was the first job he'd ever had, and he wouldn't have had it if his father hadn't insisted that if sonny wanted to keep his fingers in the family till he'd have to get over the notion that squeezing through a college graduation was enough work for one lifetime. So Jack came to the Agency. He thought gumshoeing would be fun. In spite of the fact that he'd rather catch the wrong man than wear the wrong necktie, he was a promising young thief-catcher. A likable youngster, well-muscled for all his slimness, smooth-haired, with a gentleman's face and a gentleman's manner, nervy, quick with head and hands, full of the don't-give-a-damn gaiety that belonged to his youthfulness. He was jingle-brained, of course, and needed holding, but I would rather work with him than with a lot of old-timers I knew.

Half an hour passed with nothing to interest me.

Then a boy came into Healy's from the street—a small kid, gaudily dressed, very pressed in the pants legs, very shiny in the shoes, with an impudent sallow face of pronounced cast. This was the boy I had seen sauntering down Broadway a moment after Beno had been rubbed out.

Leaning back in my chair so that a woman's wide-hatted head was between us, I watched the young Armenian wind between tables to one in a far corner, where three men sat. He spoke to them—offhand, perhaps a dozen words—and moved away to another table where a snub-nosed, black-haired man sat alone. The boy dropped into the chair facing snub-nose, spoke a few words, sneered at snub-nose's questions, and ordered a drink. When his glass was empty he crossed the room to speak to a lean buzzard-faced man, and then went out of Healy's.

I followed him out, passing the table where Jack sat with the girl, catching his eye. Outside, I saw the young Armenian half a block away.

Jack Counihan caught up with me, passed me. With a Fatima in my mouth I called to him:

"Got a match, brother?"

While I lighted my cigarette with a match from the box he gave me I spoke to him behind my hands:

"The goose in the glad rags—tail him. I'll string behind you. I don't know him, but if he blipped Beno off for talking to me last night, he knows me. On his heels!"

Jack pocketed his matches and went after the boy. I gave Jack a lead and then followed him.

And then an interesting thing happened.

The street was fairly well filled with people, mostly

men, some walking, some loafing on corners and in front of soft-drink parlors. As the young Armenian reached the corner of an alley where there was a light, two men came up and spoke to him, moving a little apart so that he was between them. The boy would have kept walking apparently paying no attention to them, but one checked him by stretching an arm out in front of him. The other man took his right hand out of his pocket and flourished it in the boy's face so that the nickel-plated knuckles on it twinkled in the light. The boy ducked swiftly under threatening hand and outstretched arm, and went on across the alley, walking, and not even looking over his shoulder at the two men who were now closing on his back.

Just before they reached him another reached them—a broad-backed, long-armed, ape-built man I had not seen before. Each hand caught a man. By the napes of their necks he yanked them away from the boy's back, shook them till their hats fell off, smacked their skulls together with a crack that was like a broom-handle breaking, and dragged their rag-limp bodies out of sight up the alley. While this was happening the boy walked jauntily down the street, without a backward glance.

When the skull-cracker came out of the alley I saw his face in the light—a dark-skinned heavily-lined face, broad and flat, with jaw muscles bulging like abscesses under his ears. He spit, hitched his pants, and swaggered down the street after the boy.

The boy went into Larrouy's. The skull-cracker followed him in. The boy came out, and in his rear—perhaps twenty feet behind—the skull-cracker rolled.

Jack had tailed them into Larrouy's while I had held up the outside.

"Still carrying messages?" I asked.

"Yes. He spoke to five men in there. He's got plenty of bodyguard, hasn't he?"

"Yeah," I agreed. "And you be damned careful you don't get between them. If they split, I'll shadow the skull-cracker, you keep the goose."

We separated and moved after our game.

They took us to all the hangouts in San Francisco, to cabarets, grease-joints, poolrooms, saloons, flop-houses, hock-shops, gambling joints and what have you. Everywhere the kid found men to speak his dozen words to, and between calls, he found them on street corners.

I would have liked to get behind some of these birds, but I didn't want to leave Jack alone with the boy and his bodyguard—they seemed to mean too much. And I couldn't stick Jack on one of the others, because it wasn't safe for me to hang too close to the Armenian boy.

So we played the game as we had started it, shadowing our pair from hole to hole, while night got on toward morning.

It was a few minutes past midnight when they came out of a small hotel up on Kearny Street, and for the first time since we had seen them they walked together, side by side, up to Green Street, where they turned east along the side of Telegraph Hill. Half a block of this, and they climbed the front steps of a ramshackle furnished-room house and disappeared inside.

I joined Jack Counihan on the corner where he had stopped.

"The greetings have all been delivered," I guessed, "or he wouldn't have called in his bodyguard. If there's nothing stirring within the next half hour I'm going to beat it. You'll have to take a plant on the joint till morning."

Twenty minutes later the skull-cracker came out of the house and walked down the street.

"I'll take him," I said. "You stick to the other baby."

The skull-cracker took ten or twelve steps from the house and stopped. He looked back at the house, raising his face to look at the upper stories.

Then Jack and I could hear what had stopped him.

Up in the house a man was screaming. It wasn't much of a scream in volume. Even now, when it had increased in strength, it barely reached our ears. But in it—in that one wailing voice—everything that fears death seemed to cry out its fear.

I heard Jack's teeth click. I've got horny skin all over what's left of my soul, but just the same my forehead twitched. The scream was so damned weak for what it said.

The skull-cracker moved. Five gliding strides carried him back to the house. He didn't touch one of the six or seven front steps. He went from pavement to vestibule in a spring no monkey could have beaten for swiftness, ease or silence.

One minute, two minutes, three minutes, and the screaming stopped. Three more minutes and the skull-cracker was leaving the house again. He paused on the sidewalk to spit and hitch his pants. Then he swaggered off down the street.

"He's your meat, Jack," I said. "I'm going to call on the boy. He won't recognize me now."

Chapter Five

The Shifty-Eyed Girl

The street door of the rooming-house was not only unlocked but wide open. I went through it into a hallway, where a dim light burning upstairs outlined a flight of steps. I climbed them and turned toward the front of the house.

The scream had come from the front—either this floor or the third. There was a fair likelihood of the skull-cracker having left the room door unlocked, just as he had not paused to close the street door.

I had no luck on the second floor, but the third knob I cautiously tried on the third floor turned in my hand and let its door edge back from the frame. In front of this crack I waited a moment, listening to nothing but a throbbing snore somewhere far down the hallway.

I put a palm against the door and eased it open another foot. No sound. The room was black as an honest politician's prospects.

I slid my hand across the frame, across a few inches of wallpaper, found a light button, pressed it. Two globes in the center of the room threw their weak yellow light on the shabby room and on the young Armenian who lay dead across the bed.

I went into the room, closed the door and stepped over to the bed.

The boy's eyes were wide and bulging. One of his temples was bruised. His throat gaped with a red slit that ran actually from ear to ear. Around the slit, in the few spots not washed red, his thin neck showed dark bruises. The skull-cracker had dropped the boy with a poke in the temple and had choked him until he thought him dead. But the kid had revived enough to scream—not enough to keep from screaming. The skull-cracker had returned to finish the job with a knife. Three streaks on the bedclothes showed where the knife had been cleaned.

The lining of the boy's pockets stuck out. The skull-cracker had turned them out. I went through his clothes, but with no better luck than I expected—the killer had taken everything. The room gave me nothing—a few clothes, but not a thing out of which information could be squeezed.

My prying done, I stood in the center of the floor scratching my chin and considering. In the hall a floor board creaked. Three backward steps on my rubber heels put me in the musty closet, dragging the door all but half an inch shut behind me.

Knuckles rattled on the room door as I slid my gun off my hip.

The knuckles rattled again and a feminine voice said, "Kid, oh, Kid!" Neither knuckles nor voice was loud.

The lock clicked as the knob turned. The door opened and framed the shifty-eyed girl who had been called Sylvia Yount by Angel Grace.

Her eyes lost their shiftiness for surprise when they settled on the boy.

"Holy hell!" she gasped, and was gone.

I was half out of the closet when I heard her tiptoeing back. In my hole again, I waited, my eye to the crack.

She came in swiftly, closed the door silently, and went to lean over the dead boy. Her hands moved over him, exploring the pockets whose linings I had put back in place.

"Damn such luck!" she said aloud when the unprofitable frisking was over, and went out of the house.

I gave her time to reach the sidewalk. She was headed toward Kearny Street when I left the house. I shadowed her down Kearny to Broadway, up Broadway to Larrouy's. Larrouy's was busy, especially near the door, with customers going and coming. I was within five feet of the girl when she stopped a waiter and asked, in a whisper that was excited enough to carry:

"Is Red here?"

The waiter shook his head.

"Ain't been in tonight."

The girl went out of the dive, hurrying along on clicking heels to a hotel in Stockton Street.

While I looked through the glass front, she went to the desk and spoke to the clerk. He shook his head. She spoke again and he gave her paper and envelope, on which she scribbled with the pen beside the register.

Before I had to leave for a safer position from which to cover her exit, I saw which pigeon-hole the note went into.

From the hotel the girl went by street-car to Market and Powell Streets, and then walked up Powell to O'Farrell, where a fat-faced young man in gray overcoat and gray hat left the curb to link arms with her and lead her to a taxi stand up O'Farrell Street.

I let them go, making a note of the taxi number—the fat-faced man looked more like a customer than a pal.

It was a little shy of two in the morning when I turned back into Market Street and went up to the office. Fiske, who holds down the Agency at night, said Jack Counihan had not reported, nothing else had come in. I told him to rouse me an operative, and in ten or fifteen minutes he succeeded in getting Mickey Linehan out of bed and on the wire.

"Listen, Mickey," I said, "I've got the nicest corner picked out for you to stand on the rest of the night. So pin on your diapers and toddle down there like a good boy, will you?"

In between his grumbling and cursing I gave him the name and number of the Stockton Street hotel, described Red O'Leary, and told him which pigeon-hole the note had been put in.

"It mightn't be Red's home, but the chance is worth covering," I wound up. "If you pick him up, try not to lose him before I can get somebody down there to take him off your hands."

I hung up during the outburst of profanity this insult brought.

The Hall of Justice was busy when I reached it, though nobody had tried to shake the upstairs prison loose yet. Fresh lots of suspicious characters were being brought in every few minutes. Policemen in and out of uniform were everywhere. The detective bureau was a beehive.

Trading information with the police detectives, I told them about the Armenian boy. We were making up a party to visit the remains when the captain's door opened and Lieutenant Duff came into the assembly room.

"Allez! Oop!" he said, pointing a thick finger at

O'Gar, Tully, Reecher, Hunt and me. "There's a thing worth looking at in Fillmore."

We followed him out to an automobile.

Chapter Six

Fourteen Plus Six

A gray frame house in Fillmore Street was our destination. A lot of people stood in the street looking at the house. A police wagon stood in front of it, and police uniforms were indoors and out.

A red-mustached corporal saluted Duff and led us into the house, explaining as we went:

" 'Twas the neighbors give us the rumble, complaining of the fighting, and when we got here, faith, there weren't no fight left in nobody."

All the house held was fourteen dead men.

Eleven of them had been poisoned—overdoses of knockout drops in their booze, the doctors said. The other three had been shot, at intervals along the hall. From the looks of the remains, they had drunk a toast—a loaded one—and those who hadn't drunk, whether because of temperance or suspicious natures, had been gunned as they tried to get away.

The identity of the bodies gave us an idea of what their toast had been. They were all thieves—they had drunk their poison to the day's looting.

We didn't know all the dead men then, but all of us knew some of them, and the records told us who the others were later. The completed list read like *Who's Who in Crookdom.*

There was the Dis-and-Dat Kid, who had crushed out of Leavenworth only two months before; Sheeny Holmes; Snohomish Shitey, supposed to have died a hero in France in 1919; L. A. Slim, from Denver, sockless and underwearless as usual, with a thousand-dollar bill sewed in each shoulder of his coat; Spider Girrucci wearing a steel-mesh vest under his shirt and a scar from crown to chin where his brother had carved him years ago; Old Pete Best, once a congressman; Nigger Vojan, who once won $175,000 in a Chicago crap game—*Abacadabra* tattooed on him in three places; Alphabet Shorty McCoy; Tom Brooks, Alphabet Shorty's brother-in-law, who invented the Richmond *razzle-dazzle,* and bought three hotels with the profits; Red Cudahy, who stuck up a Union Pacific train in 1924; Denny Burke; Bull McGonickle, still pale from fifteen years in Joliet; Toby the Lugs, Bull's running-mate, who used to brag about picking President Wilson's pocket in a Washington vaudeville theater; and Paddy the Mex.

Duff looked them over and whistled.

"A few more tricks like this," he said, "and we'll all be

out of jobs. There won't be any grifters left to protect the taxpayers from."

"I'm glad you like it," I told him. "Me—I'd hate like hell to be a San Francisco copper the next few days."

"Why especially?"

"Look at this—one grand piece of double-crossing. This village of ours is full of mean lads who are waiting right now for these stiffs to bring 'em their cut of the stick-up. What do you think's going to happen when the word gets out that there's not going to be any gravy for the mob? There are going to be a hundred and more stranded thugs busy raising getaway dough. There'll be three burglaries to a block and a stick-up to every corner until the carfare's raised. God bless you, my son, you're going to sweat for your wages!"

Duff shrugged his thick shoulders and stepped over bodies to get to the telephone. When he was through I called the Agency.

"Jack Counihan called a couple of minutes ago," Fiske told me, and gave me an Army Street address. "He says he put his men in there, with company."

I phoned for a taxi, and then told Duff:

"I'm going to run out for a while. I'll give you a ring here if there's anything to the angle, or if there isn't. You'll wait?"

"If you're not too long."

I got rid of my taxicab two blocks from the address Fiske had given me, and walked down Army Street to find Jack Counihan planted on a dark corner.

"I got a bad break," was what he welcomed me with. "While I was phoning from the lunchroom up the street some of my people ran out on me."

"Yeah? What's the dope?"

"Well, after that apey chap left the Green Street house he trolleyed to a house in Fillmore Street, and—"

"What number?"

The number Jack gave was that of the death-house I had just left.

"In the next ten or fifteen minutes just about that many other chaps went into the same house. Most of them came afoot, singly or in pairs. Then two cars came up together, with nine men in them—I counted them. They went into the house, leaving their machines in front. A taxi came past a little later, and I stopped it, in case my chap should motor away.

"Nothing happened for at least half an hour after the nine chaps went in. Then everybody in the house seemed to become demonstrative—there was a quantity of yelling and shooting. It lasted long enough to awaken the whole neighborhood. When it stopped, ten men—I counted them—ran out of the house, got into the two cars, and drove away. My man was one of them.

"My faithful taxi and I cried *Yoicks* after them, and they brought us here, going into that house down the street in front of which one of their motors still stands. After half an hour or so I thought I'd better report, so, leaving my taxi around the corner—where it's still running up expenses—I went up to Fiske. And when I came back, one of the cars was gone—and I, woe is me!—don't know who went with it. Am I rotten?"

"Sure! You should have taken their cars along to the phone with you. Watch the one that's left while I collect a strong-arm squad."

I went up to the lunchroom and phoned Duff, telling him where I was, and:

"If you bring your gang along maybe there'll be profit in it. A couple of carloads of folks who were in Fillmore Street and didn't stay there came here, and part of 'em may still be here, if you make it sudden."

Duff brought his four detectives and a dozen uniformed men with him. We hit the house front and back. No time was wasted ringing the bell. We simply tore down the doors and went in.

Everything inside was black until flashlights lit it up. There was no resistance. Ordinarily the six men we found in there would have damned near ruined us in spite of our outnumbering them. But they were too dead for that.

We looked at one another sort of open-mouthed.

"This is getting monotonous," Duff complained, biting off a hunk of tobacco. "Everybody's work is pretty much the same thing over and over, but I'm tired of walking into roomfuls of butchered crooks."

The catalog here had fewer names than the other, but they were bigger names. The Shivering Kid was here—nobody would collect all the reward money piled up on him now; Darby M'Laughlin, his horn-rimmed glasses crooked on his nose, ten thousand dollars' worth of diamonds on fingers and tie; Happy Jim Hacker; Donkey Marr, the last of the bow-legged Marrs, killers all, father and five sons; Toots Salda, the strongest man in crookdom, who had once picked up and run away with two Savannah coppers to whom he was handcuffed; and Rumdum Smith, who killed Lefty Read in Chi in 1916—a rosary wrapped around his left wrist.

No gentlemanly poisoning here—these boys had been mowed down with a .30-30 rifle fitted with a clumsy but effective homemade silencer. The rifle lay on the kitchen table. A door connected the kitchen with the dining-room. Directly opposite that door, double doors—wide open—opened into the room in which the dead thieves lay. They were all close to the front wall, lying as if they had been lined up against the wall to be knocked off.

The gray-papered wall was spattered with blood,

punctured with holes where a couple of bullets had gone all the way through. Jack Counihan's young eyes picked out a stain on the paper that wasn't accidental.

It was close to the floor, beside the Shivering Kid, and the Kid's right hand was stained with blood. He had written on the wall before he died—with fingers dipped in his own and Toots Salda's blood. The letters in the words showed breaks and gaps where his fingers had run dry, and the letters were crooked and straggly, because he must have written them in the dark.

By filling in the gaps, allowing for the kinks, and guessing where there weren't any indications to guide us, we got two words: *Big Flora.*

"They don't mean anything to me," Duff said, "but it's a name and most of the names we have belong to dead men now, so it's time we were adding to our list."

"What do you make of it?" asked bullet-headed O'Gar, detective-sergeant in the Homicide Detail, looking at the bodies. "Their pals got the drop on them, lined them against the wall, and the sharpshooter in the kitchen shot 'em down—bing-bing-bing-bing-bing-bing?"

"It reads that way," the rest of us agreed.

"Ten of 'em came here from Fillmore Street," I said. "Six stayed here. Four went to another house—where part of 'em are now cutting down the other part. All that's necessary is to trail the corpses from house to house until there's only one man left—and he's bound to play it through by croaking himself, leaving the loot to be recovered in the original packages. I hope you folks don't have to stay up all night to find the remains of that last thug. Come on, Jack, let's go home for some sleep."

Chapter Seven

A Date With Angel

It was exactly 5 a. m. when I separated the sheets and crawled into my bed. I was asleep before the last draw of smoke from my good-night Fatima was out of my lungs.

The telephone woke me at 5:15. Fiske was talking:

"Mickey Linehan just phoned that your Red O'Leary came home to roost half an hour ago."

"Have him booked," I said, and was asleep again by 5:17.

With the help of the alarm clock I rolled out of bed at nine, breakfasted, and went down to the detective bureau to see how the police had made out with the red-head. Not so good.

"He's got us stopped," the captain told me. "He's got alibis for the time of the looting and for last night's doings. And we can't even vag the son-of-a-gun. He's got means of support. He's salesman for Humperdickel's Universal Encyclopediac Dictionary of Useful and Valuable Knowledge, or something like it. He started peddling these pamphlets the day before the knock-over, and at the time it was happening he was ringing doorbells and asking folks to buy his durned books. Anyway, he's got three witnesses that say so. Last night he was in a hotel from eleven to four-thirty this morning, playing cards, and he's got witnesses. We didn't find a durned thing on him or in his room."

I borrowed the captain's phone to call Jack Counihan's house.

"Could you identify any of the men you saw in the cars last night?" I asked when he had been stirred out of bed.

"No. It was dark and they moved too fast. I could barely make sure of my chap."

"Can't, huh?" the captain said. "Well, I can hold him twenty-four hours without laying charges, and I'll do that, but I'll have to spring him unless you can dig up something."

"Suppose you turn him loose now," I suggested after thinking through my cigarette for a few minutes. "He's got himself all alibied up, so there's no reason why he should hide out on us. We'll let him alone all day—give him time to make sure he isn't being tailed—and then we'll get behind him tonight and stay behind him. Any dope on Big Flora?"

"No. That kid that was killed in Green Street was

Bernie Bernheimer, alias the Motsa Kid. I guess he was a dip—he ran with dips—but he wasn't very—"

The buzz of the phone interrupted him. He said, "Hello, yes," and "Just a minute," into the instrument, and slid it across the desk to me.

A feminine voice: "This is Grace Cardigan. I called your Agency and they told me where to get you. I've got to see you. Can you meet me now?"

"Where are you?"

"In the telephone station on Powell Street."

"I'll be there in fifteen minutes," I said.

Calling the Agency, I got hold of Dick Foley and asked him to meet me at Ellis and Market right away. Then I gave the captain back his phone, said "See you later," and went uptown to keep my dates.

Dick Foley was on his corner when I got there. He was a swarthy little Canadian who stood nearly fi
feet in his high-heeled shoes, weighed a hundred po
minus, talked like a Scotchman's telegram, and
have shadowed a drop of salt water from Go
to Hongkong without ever losing sight o

"You know Angel Grace Cardigan?

He saved a word by shaking his hea

"I'm going to meet her in the telepho
I'm through, stay behind her. She's s
be looking for you, so it won't be duck so

you can."

Dick's mouth went down at the corners and one of his rare long-winded streaks hit him.

"Harder they look, easier they are," he said.

He trailed along behind me while I went up to the station. Angel Grace was standing in the doorway. Her face was more sullen than I had ever seen it, and therefore less beautiful—except her green eyes, which held too much fire for sullenness. A rolled newspaper was in one of her hands. She neither spoke, smiled nor nodded.

"We'll go to Charley's, where we can talk," I said, guiding her down past Dick Foley.

Not a murmur did I get out of her until we were seated cross-table in the restaurant booth, and the waiter had gone off with our orders. Then she spread the newspaper out on the table with shaking hands.

"Is this on the level?" she demanded.

looked at the story her shaking finger tapped—an
nt of the Fillmore and Army Street findings, but
ccount. A glance showed that no names had
t the police had censored the story quite
retended to read I wondered whether
ny advantage to tell the girl the story
couldn't see any clear profit in that, so
a lie.

straight," I admitted.

"You were there?"

She had pushed the paper aside to the floor and was leaning over the table.

"With the police."

"Was—" Her voice broke huskily. Her white fingers wadded the tablecloth in two little bunches half-way between us. She cleared her throat. "Who was—?" was as far as she got this time.

A pause. I waited. Her eyes went down, but not before I had seen water dulling the fire in them.

During the pause the waiter came in, put our food down, went away.

"You know what I want to ask," she said presently, her voice low, choked. "Was he? Was he? For God's sake tell me!"

I weighed them—truth against lie, lie against truth. Once more truth triumphed.

"Paddy the Mex was shot—killed—in the Fillmore Street house," I said.

The pupils of her eyes shrank to pin-points—spread again until they almost covered the green irises. She made no sound. Her face was empty. She picked up a fork and lifted a forkful of salad to her mouth—another. Reaching across the table, I took the fork out of her hand.

"You're only spilling it on your clothes," I growled.

"You can't eat without opening your mouth to put the food in."

She put her hands across the table, reaching for mine, trembling, holding my hand with fingers that twitched so that the nails scratched me.

"You're not lying to me?" she half sobbed, half chattered. "You're on the square! You were white to me that time in Philly! Paddy always said you were one white dick! You're not tricking me?"

"Straight up," I assured her. "Paddy meant a lot to you?"

She nodded dully, pulling herself together, sinking back in a sort of stupor.

"The way's open to even up for him," I suggested.

"You mean—?"

"Talk."

She stared at me blankly for a long while, as if she was trying to get some meaning out of what I had said. I read the answer in her eyes before she put it in words.

"I wish to God I could! But I'm Paper-box-John Cardigan's daughter. It isn't in me to turn anybody up. You're on the wrong side. I can't go over. I wish I could. But there's too much Cardigan in me. I'll be hoping every minute that you nail them, and nail them dead right, but—"

"Your sentiments are noble, or words to that effect,"

I sneered at her. "Who do you think you are—Joan of Arc? Would your brother Frank be in stir now if his partner, Johnny the Plumber, hadn't put the finger on him for the Great Falls bulls? Come to life, dearie! You're a thief among thieves, and those who don't double-cross get crossed. Who rubbed your Paddy the Mex out? Pals! But you mustn't slap back at 'em because it wouldn't be clubby. My God!"

My speech only thickened the sullenness in her face.

"I'm going to slap back," she said, "but I can't, can't split. I can't tell you. If you were a gun, I'd—

"Anyway, what help I get will be on my side of the game. Let it go at that, won't you? I know how you feel about it, but—will you tell me who besides—who else was—was found in those houses?"

"Oh, sure!" I snarled. "I'll tell you everything. I'll let you pump me dry. But you mustn't give me any hints, because it might not be in keeping with the ethics of your highly honorable profession!"

Being a woman, she ignored all this, repeating, "Who else?"

"Nothing stirring. But I will do this—I'll tell you a couple who weren't there—Big Flora and Red O'Leary."

Her dopiness was gone. She studied my face with green eyes that were dark and savage.

"Was Bluepoint Vance?" she demanded.

"What do you guess?" I replied.

She studied my face for a moment longer and then stood up.

"Thanks for what you've told me," she said, "and for meeting me like this. I do hope you win."

She went out to be shadowed by Dick Foley. I ate my lunch.

Chapter Eight

The Wolves and the Lamb

At four o'clock that afternoon Jack Counihan and I brought our hired automobile to rest within sight of the front door of the Stockton hotel.

"He cleared himself with the police, so there's no reason why he should have moved, maybe," I told Jack, "and I'd rather not monkey with the hotel people, not knowing them. If he doesn't show by late we'll have to go up against them then."

We settled down to cigarettes, guesses on who'd be the next heavyweight champion and where to get good gin and what to do with it, the injustice of the new Agency ruling that for purposes of expense accounts Oakland was not to be considered out of town, and similar exciting topics, which carried us from four o'clock to ten minutes past nine.

At 9:10 Red O'Leary came out of the hotel.

"God is good," said Jack as he jumped out of the machine to do the footwork while I stirred the motor.

The fire-topped giant didn't take us far. Larrouy's

front door gobbled him. By the time I had parked the car and gone into the dive, both O'Leary and Jack had found seats. Jack's table was on the edge of the dance floor. O'Leary's was on the other side of the establishment, against the wall, near a corner. A fat blond couple were leaving the table back in that corner when I came in, so I persuaded the waiter who was guiding me to a table to make it that one.

O'Leary's face was three-quarters turned away from me. He was watching the front door, watching it with an earnestness that turned suddenly to happiness when a girl appeared there. She was the girl Angel Grace had called Nancy Regan. I have already said she was nice. Well, she was. And the cocky little blue hat that hid all her hair didn't handicap her niceness any tonight.

The red-head scrambled to his feet and pushed a waiter and a couple of customers out of his way as he went to meet her. As reward for his eagerness he got some profanity that he didn't seem to hear and a blue-eyed, white-toothed smile that was—well—nice. He brought her back to his table, and put her in a chair facing me, while he sat very much facing her.

His voice was a baritone rumble out of which my snooping ears could pick no words. He seemed to be telling her a lot, and she listened as if she liked it.

"But, Reddy, dear, you shouldn't," she said once.

Her voice—I know other words, but we'll stick to this one—was nice. Outside of the musk in it, it had quality. Whoever this gunman's moll was, she either had had a good start in life or had learned her stuff well. Now and then, when the orchestra came up for air, I would catch a few words, but they didn't tell me anything except that neither she nor her rowdy playmate had anything against the other.

The joint had been nearly empty when she came in. By ten o'clock it was fairly crowded, and ten o'clock is early for Larrouy's customers. I began to pay less attention to Red's girl—even if she was nice—and more to my other neighbors. It struck me that there weren't many women in sight. Checking up on that, I found damned few women in proportion to the men. Men—rat-faced men, hatchet-faced men, square-jawed men, slack-chinned men, pale men, scrawny men, funny-looking men, tough-looking men, ordinary men—sitting two to a table, four to a table, more coming in, and damned few women.

These men talked to one another, as if they weren't much interested in what they were saying. They looked casually around the joint, with eyes that were blankest when they came to O'Leary. And always those casual—bored—glances did rest on O'Leary for a second or two.

I returned my attention to O'Leary and Nancy Regan. He was sitting a little more erect in his chair than he had been, but it was an easy, supple erectness, and though his shoulders had hunched a bit, there was no stiffness in them. She said something to him. He laughed, turning his face toward the center of the room, so that he seemed to be laughing not only at what she had said, but also at these men who sat around him, waiting. It was a hearty laugh, young and careless.

The girl looked surprised for a moment, as if something in the laugh puzzled her, then she went on with whatever she was telling him. She didn't know she was sitting on dynamite, I decided. O'Leary knew. Every inch of him, every gesture, said, "I'm big, strong, young, tough and red-headed. When you boys want to do your stuff I'll be here."

Time slid by. Few couples danced. Jean Larrouy went around with dark worry in his round face. His joint was full of customers, but he would rather have had it empty.

By eleven o'clock I stood up and beckoned to Jack Counihan. He came over, we shook hands, exchanged *How's everythings* and *Getting muches,* and he sat at my table.

"What is happening?" he asked under cover of the orchestra's din. "I can't see anything, but there is something in the air. Or am I being hysterical?"

"You will be presently. The wolves are gathering, and Red O'Leary's the lamb. You could pick a tenderer one if you had a free hand, maybe. But these bimbos once helped pluck a bank, and when pay-day came there wasn't anything in their envelopes, not even any envelopes. The word got out that maybe Red knew how-come. Hence this. They're waiting now—maybe for somebody—maybe till they get enough hooch in them."

"And we sit here because it's the nearest table to the target for all these fellows' bullets when the blooming lid blows off?" Jack inquired. "Let's move over to Red's table. It's still nearer, and I rather like the appearance of the girl with him."

"Don't be impatient, you'll have your fun," I promised him. "There's no sense in having this O'Leary killed. If they bargain with him in a gentlemanly way, we'll lay off. But if they start heaving things at him, you and I are going to pry him and his girl friend loose."

"Well spoken, my hearty!" He grinned, whitening around the mouth. "Are there any details, or do we just simply and unostentatiously pry 'em loose?"

"See the door behind me, to the right? When the pop-off comes, I'm going back there and open it up. You hold the line midway between. When I yelp, you give Red whatever help he needs to get back there."

"Aye, aye!" He looked around the room at the assembled plug-uglies, moistened his lips, and looked at the hand holding his cigarette, a quivering hand. "I hope you won't think I'm in a funk," he said. "But I'm not an antique murderer like you. I get a reaction out of this prospective slaughtering."

"Reaction, my eye," I said. "You're scared stiff. But no nonsense, mind! If you try to make a vaudeville act out of it I'll ruin whatever these guerillas leave of you. You do what you're told, and nothing else. If you get any bright ideas, save 'em to tell me about afterward."

"Oh, my conduct will be most exemplary!" he assured me.

Chapter Nine

A Swell Bag of Nails

It was nearly midnight when what the wolves waited for came. The last pretense of indifference went out of faces that had been gradually taking on tenseness.

Chairs and feet scraped as men pushed themselves back a little from their tables. Muscles flexed bodies into readiness for action. Tongues licked lips and eyes looked eagerly at the front door.

Bluepoint Vance was coming into the room. He came alone, nodding to acquaintances on this side and that, carrying his tall body gracefully, easily, in its well-cut clothing. His sharp-featured face was smilingly self-confident. He came without haste and without delay to Red O'Leary's table.

I couldn't see Red's face, but muscles thickened the back of his neck. The girl smiled cordially at Vance and gave him her hand. It was naturally done. She didn't know anything.

Vance turned his smile from Nancy Regan to the red-haired giant—a smile that was a trifle cat-to-mousey.

"How's everything, Red?" he asked.

"Everything suits me," bluntly.

The orchestra had stopped playing. Larrouy, standing by the street door, was mopping his forehead with a handkerchief. At the table to my right, a barrel-chested, broken-nosed bruiser in a widely striped suit was breathing heavily between his gold teeth, his watery gray eyes bulging at O'Leary, Vance and Nancy. He was in no way conspicuous—there were too many others holding the same pose.

Bluepoint Vance turned his head, called to a waiter: "Bring me a chair."

The chair was brought and put at the unoccupied side of the table, facing the wall. Vance sat down, slumping back in the chair, leaning indolently toward Red, his left arm hooked over the chair back, his right hand holding a cigarette.

"Well, Red," he said when he was thus installed, "have you got any news for me?"

His voice was suave, but loud enough for those at near-by tables to hear.

"Not a word."

O'Leary's voice made no pretense of friendliness, nor of caution.

"What, no spinach?" Vance's thin-lipped smile spread, and his dark eyes had a mirthful but not pleasant glitter. "Nobody gave you anything to give me?"

"No," said O'Leary, emphatically.

"My goodness!" said Vance, the smile in his eyes and mouth deepening, and getting still less pleasant. "That's ingratitude! Will you help me collect, Red?"

"No."

I was disgusted with this red-head—half-minded to let him go under when the storm broke. Why couldn't he have stalled his way out—fixed up a fancy tale that Bluepoint would have had to half-way accept? But no—this O'Leary boy was so damned childishly proud of his toughness that he had to make a show of it when he should have been using his bean.

If it had been only his own carcass that was due for a beating, it would have been all right. But it wasn't all right that Jack and I should have to suffer. This big chump was too valuable to lose. We'd have to get ourselves all battered up saving him from the rewards of his own pig-headedness. There was no justice in it.

"I've a lot of money coming to me, Red." Vance spoke lazily, tauntingly. "And I need that money." He drew on his cigarette, casually blew the smoke into the red-head's face, and drawled, "Why, do you know the laundry charges twenty-six cents just for doing a pair of pajamas? I need money."

"Sleep in your underclothes," said O'Leary.

Vance laughed.

Nancy Regan smiled, but in a bewildered way. She didn't seem to know what it was all about, but she couldn't help knowing that it was about something.

O'Leary leaned forward and spoke deliberately, loud enough for any to hear:

"Bluepoint, I've got nothing to give you—now or ever. And that goes for anybody else that's interested. If you or them think I owe you something—try and get it. To hell with you, Bluepoint Vance! If you don't like it—you've got friends here. Call 'em on!"

What a prime young idiot! Nothing would suit him but an ambulance—and I must be dragged along with him.

Vance grinned evilly, his eyes glittering into O'Leary's face.

"You'd like that, Red?"

O'Leary hunched his big shoulders and let them drop.

"I don't mind a fight," he said. "But I'd like to get Nancy out of it." He turned to her. "Better run along, honey, I'm going to be busy."

She started to say something, but Vance was talking to her. His words were lightly spoken, and he made no objection to her going. The substance of what he told her was that she was going to be lonely without Red. But he went intimately into the details of that loneliness.

Red O'Leary's right hand rested on the table. It went up to Vance's mouth. The hand was a fist when it got there.

A wallop of that sort is awkward to deliver. The body can't give it much. It has to depend on the arm muscles, and not on the best of those. Yet Bluepoint Vance was driven out of his chair and across to the next table.

Larrouy's chairs went empty. The shindig was on.

"On your toes," I growled at Jack Counihan, and, doing my best to look like the nervous little fat man I was, I ran toward the back door, passing men who were moving not yet swiftly toward O'Leary.

I must have looked the part of a scared trouble-dodger, because nobody stopped me, and I reached the door before the pack had closed on Red.

The door was closed, but not locked. I wheeled with my back to it, black-jack in right hand, gun in left. Men were in front of me, but their backs were to me.

O'Leary was towering in front of his table, his tough red face full of bring-on-your-hell, his big body balanced on the balls of his feet. Between us, Jack Counihan stood, his face turned to me, his mouth twitching in a nervous grin, his eyes dancing with delight.

Bluepoint Vance was on his feet again. Blood trickled from his thin lips, down his chin. His eyes were cool. They looked at Red O'Leary with the businesslike look of a logger sizing up the tree he's going to bring down. Vance's mob watched Vance.

"Red!" I bawled into the silence. "This way, Red!"

Faces spun to me—every face in the joint—millions of them.

"Come on, Red!" Jack Counihan yelped, taking a step forward, his gun out.

Bluepoint Vance's hand flashed to the V of his coat. Jack's gun snapped at him. Bluepoint had thrown himself down before the boy's trigger was yanked. The bullet went wide, but Vance's draw was gummed.

Red scooped the girl up with his left arm. A big automatic blossomed in his right fist. I didn't pay much attention to him after that. I was busy.

Larrouy's home was pregnant with weapons—guns, knives, saps, knucks, club-swung chairs and bottles, miscellaneous implements of destruction.

Men brought their weapons over to mingle with me. The game was to nudge me away from my door. O'Leary would have liked it. But I was no fire-haired young rowdy. I was pushing forty, and I was twenty pounds overweight. I had the liking for ease that goes with that age and weight. Little ease I got.

A squint-eyed Portuguese slashed at my neck with a knife that spoiled my necktie. I caught him over the ear with the side of my gun before he could get away, saw the ear tear loose.

A grinning kid of twenty went down for my legs—football stuff. I felt his teeth in the knee I pumped up, and felt them break.

A pock-marked mulatto pushed a gun-barrel over the shoulder of the man in front of him. My blackjack crunched the arm of the man in front. He winced sidewise as the mulatto pulled the trigger—and had the side of his face blown away.

I fired twice—once when a gun was leveled within a foot of my middle, once when I discovered a man standing on a table not far off taking careful aim at my head. For the rest I trusted to my arms and legs, and saved bullets. The night was young and I had only a dozen pills—six in the gun, six in my pocket.

It was a swell bag of nails. Swing right, swing left, kick, swing right, swing left, kick. Don't hesitate, don't look for targets. God will see that there's always a mug there for your gun or blackjack to sock, a belly for your foot.

A bottle came through and found my forehead. My hat saved me some, but the crack didn't do me any good. I swayed and broke a nose where I should have smashed a skull.

The room seemed stuffy, poorly ventilated. Somebody ought to tell Larrouy about it. How do you like that lead-and-leather pat on the temple, blondy? This rat on my left is getting too close. I'll draw him in by bending to the right to poke the mulatto, and then I'll lean back into him and let him have it.

Not bad! But I can't keep this up all night. Where are Red and Jack? Standing off watching me?

Somebody socked me in the shoulder with something—a piano from the feel of it. I couldn't miss it. Another thrown bottle took my hat and part of my scalp.

Red O'Leary and Jack Counihan smashed through, dragging the girl between them.

Chapter Ten

Red's Girl

While Jack put the girl through the door, Red and I cleared a little space in front of us. He was good at that. I didn't dog it on him, but I did let him get all the exercise he wanted.

"All right!" Jack called.

Red and I went through the door, slammed it shut. It wouldn't hold even if locked. O'Leary sent three slugs through it to give the boys something to think about, and our retreat got under way.

We were in a narrow passageway lighted by a fairly bright light. At the other end was a closed door. Halfway down, to the right, steps led up.

"Straight ahead?" asked Jack, who was in front.

O'Leary said, "Yes," and I said, "No. Vance will have that blocked by now if the bulls haven't. Upstairs—the roof."

We reached the stairs. The door behind us burst open. The light went out. The door at the other end of the passage slammed open. No light came through either door. Vance would want light. Larrouy must have pulled the switch, trying to keep his dump from being torn to toothpicks.

Tumult boiled in the dark passage as we climbed the stairs by the touch system. Whoever had come through the back door was mixing it with those who had followed us—mixing it with blows, curses and an occasional shot.

More power to them! We climbed, Jack leading, the girl next, then me, and last of all, O'Leary.

Jack was gallantly reading road-signs to the girl:

"Careful of the landing, half a turn to the left now, put your right hand on the wall and—"

"Shut up!" I growled at him. "It's better to have her falling down than to have everybody in the drum fall on us."

We reached the second floor. It was black as black. There were three stories to the building.

"I've mislaid the blooming stairs," Jack complained.

We poked around clumsily in the dark, hunting for the flight that should lead up toward the roof. We didn't find it.

The riot downstairs was quieting. Vance's voice was telling his push that they were mixing it with each other, asking where we had gone. Nobody seemed to know. We didn't know, either.

"Come on," I grumbled, leading the way down the dark hall toward the back of the building. "We've got to go somewhere."

There was still noise downstairs, but no more fighting. Men were talking about getting lights. I stumbled into a door at the end of the hall, pushed it open. A room with two windows through which came a pale glow from the street lights. It seemed brilliant after the hall. My little flock followed me in and we closed the door.

Red O'Leary was across the room, his noodle to an open window.

"Back street," he whispered. "No way down unless we drop."

"Anybody in sight?" I asked.

"Don't see any."

I looked around the room—bed, couple of chairs, chest of drawers, and a table.

"The table will go through the window," I said. "We'll chuck it as far as we can and hope the racket will lead 'em out there before they decide to look up here."

Red and the girl were assuring each other that each was still all in one piece. He broke away from her to help me with the table. We balanced it, swung it, let it go. It did nicely, crashing into the wall of the building opposite, dropping down into a backyard to clang and clatter on a pile of tin, or a collection of garbage cans, or something beautifully noisy. You couldn't have heard it more than a block and a half away.

We got away from the window as men bubbled out of Larrouy's back door.

The girl, unable to find any wounds on O'Leary, had turned to Jack Counihan. He had a cut cheek. She was monkeying with it and a handkerchief.

"When you finish that," Jack was telling her, "I'm going out and get one on the other side."

"I'll never finish if you keep talking—you jiggle your cheek."

"That's a swell idea," he exclaimed. "San Francisco is the second largest city in California. Sacramento is the State capital. Do you like geography? Shall I tell you about Java? I've never been there, but I drink their coffee. If—"

"Silly!" she said, laughing. "If you don't hold still I'll stop now."

"Not so good," he said. "I'll be still."

She wasn't doing anything except wiping blood off his cheek, blood that had better been let dry there. When she finished this perfectly useless surgery, she took her hand away slowly, surveying the hardly noticeable results with pride. As her hand came on a level with his mouth, Jack jerked his head forward to kiss the tip of one passing finger.

"Silly!" she said again, snatching her hand away.

"Lay off that," said Red O'Leary, "or I'll knock you off."

"Pull in your neck," said Jack Counihan.

"Reddy!" the girl cried too late.

The O'Leary right looped out. Jack took the punch on the button, and went to sleep on the floor. The big red-head spun on the balls of his feet to loom over me.

"Got anything to say?" he asked.

I grinned down at Jack, up at Red.

"I'm ashamed of him," I said. "Letting himself be stopped by a paluka who leads with his right."

"You want to try it?"

"Reddy! Reddy!" the girl pleaded, but nobody was listening to her.

"If you'll lead with your right," I said.

"I will," he promised, and did.

I grandstanded, slipping my head out of the way, laying a forefinger on his chin.

"That could have been a knuckle," I said.

"Yes? This one is."

I managed to get under his left, taking the forearm across the back of my neck. But that about played out the acrobatics. It looked as if I would have to see what I could do to him, if any.

The girl grabbed his arm and hung on.

"Reddy, darling, haven't you had enough fighting for one night? Can't you be sensible, even if you are Irish?"

I was tempted to paste the big chew while his playmate had him tied up.

He laughed down at her, ducked his head to kiss her mouth, and grinned at me.

"There's always some other time," he said good-naturedly.

Chapter Eleven

Bulldozing a Man

"We'd better get out of here if we can," I said. "You've made too much rumpus for it to be safe."

"Don't get it up in your neck, little man," he told me. "Hold on to my coat-tails and I'll pull you out."

The big tramp. If it hadn't been for Jack and me he wouldn't have had any coat-tail by now.

We moved to the door, listened there, heard nothing.

"The stairs to the third floor must be up front," I whispered. "We'll try for them now."

We opened the door carefully. Enough light went past us into the hall to show a promise of emptiness. We crept down the hall, Red and I each holding one of the girl's hands. I hoped Jack would come out all right, but he had put himself to sleep, and I had troubles of my own.

I hadn't known that Larrouy's was large enough to have two miles of hall-way. It did. It was an even mile in the darkness to the head of the stairs we had come up. We didn't pause there to listen to the voices below. At the end of the next mile O'Leary's foot found the bottom step of the flight leading up.

Just then a yell broke out at the head of the other flight.

"All up—they're up here!"

A white light beamed up on the yeller, and a brogue addressed him from below:

"Come on down, ye windbag."

"The police," Nancy Regan whispered, and we hustled up our new-found steps to the third floor.

More darkness, just like that we'd left. We stood still at the top of the stairs. We didn't seem to have any company.

"The roof," I said. "We'll risk matches."

Back in a corner our feeble match-light found us a ladder nailed to the wall, leading to a trap in the ceiling. As little later as possible we were on Larrouy's roof, the trap closed behind us.

"All silk so far," said O'Leary, "and if Vance's rats and the bulls will play a couple of seconds longer—bingavast."

I led the way across the roofs. We dropped ten feet to the next building, climbed a bit to the next, and found on the other side of it a fire-escape that ran down to a narrow court with an opening into the back street.

"This ought to do it," I said, and went down.

The girl came behind me, and then Red. The court into which we dropped was empty—a narrow cement passage between buildings. The bottom of the fire-escape creaked as it hinged down under my weight, but the noise didn't stir anything. It was dark in the court, but not black.

"When we hit the street, we split," O'Leary told me, without a word of gratitude for my help—the help he didn't seem to know he had needed. "You roll your hoop, we'll roll ours."

"Uh-huh," I agreed, chasing my brains around in my skull. "I'll scout the alley first."

Carefully I picked my way down to the end of the court and risked the top of my hatless head to peep into the back street.

It was quiet, but at the corner, a quarter of a block above, two loafers seemed to be loafing attentively. They weren't coppers. I stepped out into the back street and beckoned them. They couldn't recognize me at that distance, in that light, and there was no reason why they shouldn't think me one of Vance's crew, if they belonged to him.

As they came toward me I stepped back into the court and hissed for Red. He wasn't a boy you had to call twice to a row. He got to me just as they arrived. I took one. He took the other.

Because I wanted a disturbance, I had to work like a mule to get it. These bimbos were a couple of lollipops for fair. There wouldn't have been an ounce of fight in a ton of them. The one I had didn't know what to make of my roughing him around. He had a gun, but he managed to drop it first thing, and in the wrestling it got kicked out of reach. He hung on while I sweated ink jockeying him around into position. The darkness helped, but even at that it was no cinch to pretend he was putting up a battle while I worked him around behind O'Leary, who wasn't having any trouble at all with his man.

Finally I made it. I was behind O'Leary, who had his man pinned against the wall with one hand, preparing to sock him again with the other.

I clamped my left hand on my playmate's wrist, twisted him to his knees, got my gun out, and shot O'Leary in the back, just below the right shoulder.

Red swayed, jamming his man into the wall. I beaned mine with the gun-butt.

"Did he get you, Red?" I asked, steadying him with an arm, knocking his prisoner across the noodle.

"Yeah."

"Nancy," I called.

She ran to us.

"Take his other side," I told her. "Keep on your feet,

Red, and we'll make the sneak O. K."

The bullet was too freshly in him to slow him up yet, though his right arm was out of commission. We ran down the back street to the corner.

We had pursuers before we made it. Curious faces looked at us in the street. A policeman a block away began to move our way. The girl helping O'Leary on one side, me on the other, we ran half a block away from the copper, to where I had left the automobile Jack and I had used. The street was active by the time I got the machinery grinding and the girl had Red stowed safely in the back seat.

The copper sent a yell and a high bullet after us. We left the neighborhood.

I didn't have any special destination yet, so, after the necessary first burst of speed, I slowed up a little, went around lots of corners, and brought the bus to rest in a dark street beyond Van Ness Avenue.

Red was drooping in one corner of the back, the girl holding him up, when I screwed around in my seat to look at them.

"Where to?" I asked.

"A hospital, a doctor, something!" the girl cried. "He's dying!"

I didn't believe that. If he was, it was his own fault. If he had had enough gratitude to take me along with him as a friend I wouldn't have had to shoot him so I could go along as nurse.

"Where to, Red?" I asked him, prodding his knee with a finger.

He spoke thickly, giving me the address of the Stockton Street hotel.

"That's no good," I objected. "Everybody in town knows you bunk there, and if you go back, it's lights out for yours. Where to?"

"Hotel," he repeated.

I got up, knelt on the seat, and leaned back to work on him. He was weak. He couldn't have much resistance left. Bulldozing a man who might after all be dying wasn't gentlemanly, but I had invested a lot of trouble in this egg, trying to get him to lead me to his friends, and I wasn't going to quit in the stretch.

For a while it looked as if he wasn't weak enough yet, as if I'd have to shoot him again. But the girl sided with me, and between us we finally convinced him that his only safe bet was to go somewhere where he could hide while he got the right kind of care. We didn't actually convince him—we wore him out and he gave in because he was too weak to argue longer. He gave me an address out by Holly Park.

Hoping for the best, I pointed the machine thither.

Chapter Twelve

Big Flora

The house was a small one in a row of small houses. We took the big boy out of the car and between us to the door. He could just about make it with our help.

The street was dark. No light showed from the house. I rang the bell.

Nothing happened. I rang again, and then once more.

"Who is it?" a harsh voice demanded from the inside.

"Red's been hurt," I said.

Silence for a while. Then the door opened half a foot. Through the opening a light came from the interior, enough light to show the flat face and bulging jaw-muscles of the skull-cracker who had been the Motsa Kid's guardian and executioner.

"What the hell?" he asked.

"Red was jumped. They got him," I explained, pushing the limp giant forward.

We didn't crash the gate that way. The skull-cracker held the door as it was.

"You'll wait," he said, and shut the door in our faces.

His voice sounded from within, "Flora."

That was all right—Red had brought us to the right place.

When he opened the door again he opened it all the way, and Nancy Regan and I took our burden into the hall. Beside the skull-cracker stood a woman in a low-cut black silk gown—Big Flora, I supposed.

She stood at least five feet ten in her high-heeled slippers. They were small slippers, and I noticed that her ringless hands were small. The rest of her wasn't. She was broad-shouldered, deep-bosomed, thick-armed, with a pink throat which, for all its smoothness was muscled like a wrestler's. She was about my age—close to forty—with very curly and very yellow bobbed hair, very pink skin, and a handsome, brutal face. Her deep-set eyes were gray, her thick lips were well-shaped, her nose was just broad enough and curved enough to give her a look of strength, and she had chin enough to support it.

From forehead to throat her pink skin was underlaid with smooth, thick, strong muscles.

This Big Flora was no toy. She had the look and the poise of a woman who could have managed the looting and the double-crossing afterward. Unless her face and body lied, she had all the strength of physique, mind and will that would be needed, and some to spare. She was made of stronger stuff than either the ape-built bruiser at her side or the red-haired giant I was holding.

"Well?" she asked, when the door had been closed behind us.

Her voice was deep but not masculine—a voice that went well with her looks.

"Vance ganged him in Larrouy's. He took one in the back," I said.

"Who are you?"

"Get him to bed," I stalled. "We've got all night to talk."

She turned, snapping her fingers. A shabby little old man darted out of a door toward the rear. His brown eyes were very scary.

"Get to hell upstairs," she ordered. "Fix the bed, get hot water and towels."

The little old man scrambled up the stairs like a rheumatic rabbit.

The skull-cracker took the girl's side of Red, and he and I carried the giant up to a room where the little man was scurrying around with basins and cloth. Flora and Nancy Regan followed us.

We spread the wounded man face-down on the bed and stripped him. Blood still ran from the bullet-hole. He was unconscious.

Nancy Regan went to pieces.

"He's dying! Get a doctor! Oh, Reddy, dearest—"

"Shut up!" said Big Flora. "The damned fool ought to croak—going to Larrouy's tonight!" She caught the little man by the shoulder and threw him at the door. "Zonite and more water," she called after him. "Give me your knife, Pogy."

The ape-built man took from his pocket a spring-knife with a long blade that had been sharpened until it was narrow and thin. This is the knife, I thought, that cut the Motsa Kid's throat.

With it, Big Flora cut the bullet out of Red O'Leary's back.

The ape-built Pogy kept Nancy Regan over in a corner of the room while the operating was done. The little scared man knelt beside the bed, handing the woman what she asked for, mopping up Red's blood as it ran from the wound.

I stood beside Flora, smoking cigarettes from the pack she had given me. When she raised her head, I would transfer the cigarette from my mouth to hers. She would fill her lungs with a draw that ate half the cigarette and nod. I would take the cigarette from her mouth. She would blow out the smoke and bend to her work again.

I would light another cigarette from what was left of that one, and be ready for her next smoke.

Her bare arms were blood to the elbows. Her face was damp with sweat. It was a gory mess, and it took time. But when she straightened up for the last smoke, the bullet was out of Red, the bleeding had stopped, and he was bandaged.

"Thank God that's over," I said, lighting one of my own cigarettes. "Those pills you smoke are terrible."

The little scared man was cleaning up. Nancy Regan had fainted in a chair across the room, and nobody was paying any attention to her.

"Keep your eye on this gent, Pogy," Big Flora told the skull-cracker, nodding at me, "while I wash up."

I went over to the girl, rubbed her hands, put some water on her face, and got her awake.

"The bullet's out. Red's sleeping. He'll be picking fights again within a week," I told her.

She jumped up and ran over to the bed.

Flora came in. She had washed and had changed her blood-stained black gown for a green kimono affair, which gaped here and there to show a lot of orchid-colored underthings.

"Talk," she commanded, standing in front of me. "Who, what and why?"

"I'm Percy Maguire," I said, as if this name, which I had just thought up, explained everything.

"That's the who," she said, as if my phony alias explained nothing. "Now what's the what and why?"

The ape-built Pogy, standing on one side, looked me up and down.

I'm short and lumpy. My face doesn't scare children, but it's a more or less truthful witness to a life that hasn't been overburdened with refinement and gentility. The evening's entertainment had decorated me with bruises and scratches, and had done things to what was left of my clothes.

"Percy," he echoed, showing wide-spaced yellow teeth in a grin. "My Gawd, brother, your folks must of been color-blind!"

"That's the what and why," I insisted to the woman, paying no attention to the wheeze from the zoo. "I'm Percy Maguire, and I want my hundred and fifty thousand dollars."

The muscles in her brows came down over her eyes.

"You've got a hundred and fifty thousand dollars, have you?"

I nodded up into her handsome brutal face.

"Yeah," I said. "That's what I came for."

"Oh, you haven't got them? You want them?"

"Listen, sister, I want my dough." I had to get tough if this play was to go over. "This swapping *Oh-have-yous* and *Yes-I-haves* don't get me anything but a thirst. We were in the big knock-over, see? And after that, when we find the pay-off's a bust, I said to the kid I was training with, 'Never mind, Kid, we'll get our whack. Just follow Percy.' And then Bluepoint comes to me to throw in with him, and I said, 'Sure' and me and the kid throw in with him until we all come across Red in the dump tonight. Then I told the kid, 'These coffee-and-doughnut guns are going to rub Red out, and that won't get us anything. We'll take him away from 'em and make him steer us to where Big Flora's sitting on the jack. We ought to be good for a hundred and fifty grand apiece, now that there's damned few in on it. After we get that, if we want to bump Red off, all right. But business before pleasure, and a hundred and fifty thou is business.' So we did. We opened an out for the big boy when he didn't have any. The kid got mushy with the broad along the road and got knocked for a loop. That was all right with me. If she was worth a hundred and fifty grand to him—fair enough. I came on with Red. I pulled the big tramp out after he stopped the slug. By rights I ought to collect the kid's dib, too—making three hundred thou for me—but give me the hundred and fifty I started out for and we'll call it even-steven."

I thought this hocus ought to stick. Of course I wasn't counting on her ever giving me any money, but if the rank and file of the mob hadn't known these people, why should these people know everybody in the mob?

Flora spoke to Pogy:

"Get that damned heap away from the front door."

I felt better when he went out. She wouldn't have sent him out to move the car if she had meant to do anything to me right away.

"Got any food in the joint?" I asked, making myself at home.

She went to the head of the steps and yelled down, "Get something for us to eat."

Red was still unconscious. Nancy Regan sat beside him, holding one of his hands. Her face was drained white.

Big Flora came into the room again, looked at the invalid, put a hand on his forehead, felt his pulse.

"Come on downstairs," she said.

"I—I'd rather stay here, if I may," Nancy Regan said.

Voice and eyes showed utter terror of Flora.

The big woman, saying nothing, went downstairs. I followed her to the kitchen, where the little man was working on ham and eggs at the range. The window and back door, I saw, were reinforced with heavy planking and braced with timbers nailed to the floor. The clock over the sink said 2:50 a.m.

Flora brought out a quart of liquor and poured drinks for herself and me. We sat at the table and while we waited for our food she cursed Red O'Leary and Nancy Regan, because he had got himself disabled keeping a date with her at a time when Flora needed his strength most. She cursed them individually, as a pair, and was making it a racial matter by cursing all the Irish when the little man gave us our ham and eggs.

We had finished the solids and were stirring hooch in our second cups of coffee when Pogy came back. He had news.

"There's a couple of mugs hanging around the corner that I don't much like."

"Bulls or—?" Flora asked.

"Or," he said.

Flora began to curse Red and Nancy again. But she had pretty well played that line out already. She turned to me.

"What the hell did you bring them here for?" she demanded. "Leaving a mile-wide trail behind you! Why didn't you let the lousy bum die where he got his dose?"

"I brought him here for my hundred and fifty grand. Slip it to me and I'll be on my way. You don't owe me anything else. I don't owe you anything. Give me my rhino instead of lip and I'll pull my freight."

"Like hell you will," said Pogy.

The woman looked at me under lowered brows and drank her coffee.

Chapter Thirteen

Talking Turkey

Fifteen minutes later the shabby little old man came running into the kitchen, saying he had heard feet on the roof. His faded brown eyes were dull as an ox's with fright, and his withered lips writhed under his straggly, yellow-white mustache.

Flora profanely called him a this-and-that kind of old one-thing-and-another and chased him upstairs again. She got up from the table and pulled the green kimono tight around her big body.

"You're here," she told me, "and you'll put in with us. There's no other way. Got a rod?"

I admitted I had a gun but shook my head at the rest of it.

"This is not my wake—yet," I said. "It'll take one hundred and fifty thousand berries, spot cash, paid in the hand, to buy Percy in on it."

I wanted to know if the loot was on the premises.

Nancy Regan's tearful voice came from the stairs:

"No, no, darling! Please, please, go back to bed! You'll

kill yourself, Reddy, dear!"

Red O'Leary strode into the kitchen. He was naked except for a pair of gray pants and his bandage. His eyes were feverish and happy. His dry lips were stretched in a grin. He had a gun in his left hand. His right arm hung useless.

Behind him trotted Nancy. She stopped pleading and shrank behind him when she saw Big Flora.

"Ring the gong, and let's go," the half-naked red-head laughed. "Vance is in our street."

Flora went over to him, put her fingers on his wrist, held them there a couple of seconds, and nodded:

"You crazy son-of-a-gun," she said in a tone that was more like maternal pride than anything else. "You're good for a fight right now. And a damned good thing, too, because you're going to get it."

Red laughed—a triumphant laugh that boasted of his toughness—then his eyes turned to me. Laughter went out of them and a puzzled look drew them narrow.

"Hello," he said. "I dreamed about you, but I can't remember what it was. It was—Wait. I'll get it in a minute. It was—By God! I dreamed it was you that plugged me!"

Flora smiled at me, the first time I had seen her smile, and she spoke quickly:

"Take him, Pogy!"

I twisted obliquely out of my chair.

Pogy's fist took me in the temple. Staggering across the room, struggling to keep my feet, I thought of the bruise on the dead Motsa Kid's temple.

Pogy was on me when the wall bumped me upright.

I put a fist—spat!—in his flat nose. Blood squirted, but his hairy paws gripped me. I tucked my chin in, ground the top of my head into his face.

The scent Big Flora used came strong to me. Her silk clothes brushed against me. With both hands full of my hair she pulled my head back, stretching my neck for Pogy. He took hold of it with his paws.

I quit. He didn't throttle me any more than was necessary, but it was bad enough.

Flora frisked me for a gun and blackjack.

".38 special," she named the caliber of the gun. "I dug a .38 special bullet out of you, Red."

The words came faintly to me through the roaring in my ears.

The little old man's voice was chattering in the kitchen. I couldn't make out anything he said. Pogy's hands went away from me. I put my own hands to my throat. It was hell not to have any pressure at all there. The blackness went slowly away from my eyes, leaving a lot of little purple clouds that floated around and around. Presently I could sit up on the floor. I knew by that I had been lying down on it.

The purple clouds shrank until I could see past them enough to know there were only three of us in the room now.

Cringing in a chair, back in a corner, was Nancy Regan. On another chair, beside the door, a black pistol in his hand, sat the scared little old man. His eyes were desperately frightened. Gun and hand shook at me. I tried to ask him to either stop shaking or move his gun away from me, but I couldn't get any words out yet.

Upstairs, guns boomed, their reports exaggerated by the smallness of the house.

The little man winced.

"Let me get out," he whispered with unexpected abruptness, "and I will give you everything. I will! Everything—if you will let me get out of this house!"

This feeble ray of light where there hadn't been a dot gave me back the use of my vocal apparatus.

"Talk turkey," I managed to say.

"I will give you those upstairs—that she-devil. I will give you the money, I will give you all—if you will let me go out. I am old. I am sick. I cannot live in prison. What have I to do with robberies? Nothing. Is it my fault that she-devil—? You have seen it here. I am a slave—I who am near the end of my life. Abuse, cursings, beatings—and those are not enough. Now I must go to prison because that she-devil is a she-devil. I am an old man who cannot live in prisons. You let me go out. You do me that kindness. I will give you that she-devil—those other devils—the money they stole. That I will do!"

Thus this panic-stricken little old man squirming and fidgeting on his chair.

"How can I get you out?" I asked, getting up from the floor, my eye on his gun.

If I could get to him while we talked.

"How not? You are a friend of the police—that I know. The police are here now—waiting for daylight before they come into this house. I myself with my old eyes saw them take Bluepoint Vance. You can take me out past your friends, the police. You do what I ask, and I will give you those devils and their moneys."

"Sounds good," I said, taking a careless step toward him. "But can I just stroll out of here when I want to?"

"No! No!" he said, paying no attention to the second step I took toward him. "But first I will give you those three devils. I will give them to you alive but without power. And their money. That I will do, and then you will take me out—and this girl here." He nodded suddenly at Nancy, whose white face, still nice in spite of its terror, was mostly wide eyes just now. "She, too, has nothing to do with those devils' crimes. She must go with me."

I wondered what this old rabbit thought he could do. I frowned, exceedingly thoughtful while I took still another step toward him.

"Make no mistake," he whispered earnestly. "When that she-devil comes back into this room you will die—she will kill you certainly."

Three more steps and I would be close enough to take hold of him and his gun.

Footsteps were in the hall. Too late for a jump.

"Yes?" he hissed desperately.

I nodded a split-second before Big Flora came through the door.

Chapter Fourteen

GUMMY AROUND THE EDGES

SHE WAS DRESSED for action in a pair of blue pants that were probably Pogy's, beaded moccasins, a silk waist. A ribbon held her curly yellow hair back from her face. She had a wicked-looking gun in one hand, one in each hip pocket.

The one in her hand swung up.

"You're done," she told me, quite matter-of-fact.

My newly acquired confederate whined, "Wait, wait, Flora! Not here like this, please! Let me take him into the cellar."

She scowled at him, shrugging her silken shoulders.

"Make it quick," she said. "It'll be light in another half-hour."

I felt too much like crying to laugh at them. Was I supposed to think this woman would let the rabbit change her plans? I suppose I must have put some value on the old gink's help, or I wouldn't have been so disappointed when this little comedy told me it was a frame-up. But any hole they worked me into couldn't be any worse than the one I was in.

So I went ahead of the old man into the hall, opened the door he indicated, switched on the basement light, and went down the rough steps.

Behind me he was whispering, "I'll first show you the moneys, and then I will give you those devils. And you will not forget your promise? I and that girl shall go out through the police?"

"Oh, yes," I assured the old joker.

He came up beside me, sticking a gun-butt in my hand.

"Hide it," he hissed, and, when I had pocketed that one, gave me another, producing them with his free hand from under his coat.

Then he actually showed me the loot. It was still in the boxes and bags in which it had been carried from the banks. He insisted on opening some of them to show me the money—green bundles belted with the bank's yellow wrappers. The boxes and bags were stacked in a small brick cell that was fitted with a padlocked door, to which he had the key.

He closed the door when we were through looking, but he did not lock it, and he led me back part of the way we had come.

"That, as you see, is the money," he said. "Now for those. You will stand here, hiding behind these boxes."

A partition divided the cellar in half. It was pierced by a doorway that had no door. The place the old man told me to hide was close beside this doorway, between the partition and four packing cases. Hiding there, I would be to the right of, and a little behind, anyone who came downstairs and walked through the cellar toward the cell that held the money. That is, I would be in that position when they went to go through the doorway in the partition.

The old man was fumbling beneath one of the boxes. He brought out an eighteen-inch length of lead pipe stuffed in a similar length of black garden hose. He gave this to me as he explained everything.

"They will come down here one at a time. When they are about to go through this door, you will know what to do with this. And then you will have them, and I will have your promise. Is it not so?"

"Oh, yes," I said, all up in the air.

He went upstairs. I crouched behind the boxes, examining the guns he had given me—and I'm damned if I could find anything wrong with them. They were loaded and they seemed to be in working order. That finishing touch completely balled me up. I didn't know whether I was in a cellar or a balloon.

When Red O'Leary, still naked except for pants and bandage, came into the cellar, I had to shake my head violently to clear it in time to bat him across the back of the noodle as his first bare foot stepped through the doorway. He sprawled down on his face.

The old man scurried down the steps, full of grins.

"Hurry! Hurry!" he panted, helping me drag the red-head back into the money cell.

Then he produced two pieces of cord and tied the giant hand and foot.

"Hurry!" he panted again as he left me to run upstairs, while I went back to my hiding-place and hefted the lead pipe, wondering if Flora had shot me and I was now enjoying the rewards of my virtue—in a heaven where I could enjoy myself forever and ever socking folks who had been rough with me down below.

The ape-built skull-cracker came down, reached the door. I cracked his skull. The little man came scurrying. We dragged Pogy to the cell, tied him up.

"Hurry!" panted the old gink, dancing up and down in his excitement. "That she-devil next—and strike hard!"

He scrambled upstairs and I could hear his feet pattering overhead.

I got rid of some of my bewilderment, making room for a little intelligence in my skull. This foolishness we were up to wasn't so. It couldn't be happening. Nothing ever worked out just that way. You didn't stand in corners and knock down people one after the other like a machine, while a scrawny little bozo up at the other end fed them to you.

It was too damned silly! I had enough!

I passed up my hiding-place, put down the pipe and found another spot to crouch in, under some shelves, near the steps. I hunkered down there with a gun in each fist. This game I was playing in was—it had to be—gummy around the edges. I wasn't going to stay put any longer.

Flora came down the steps. Behind her trotted the little man.

Flora had a gun in each hand. Her gray eyes were everywhere. Her head was down like an animal's coming to a fight. Her nostrils quivered. Her body, coming down neither slowly nor swiftly, was balanced like a dancer's.

If I live to a million I'll never forget the picture this handsome brutal woman made coming down those unplaned cellar stairs. She was a beautiful fight-bred animal going to a fight.

She saw me as I straightened.

"Drop 'em!" I said, but I knew she wouldn't.

The little man flicked a limp brown blackjack out of his sleeve and knocked her behind the ear just as she swung her left gun on me.

I jumped over and caught her before she hit the cement.

"Now, you see!" the old man said gleefully. "You have the money and you have them. And now you will get me and that girl out."

"First we'll stow this with the others," I said.

After he had helped me do that I told him to lock the cell door. He did, and I took the key with one hand, his neck with the other. He squirmed like a snake while I ran my other hand over his clothes, removing the black-jack and a gun, and finding a money-belt around his waist.

"Take it off," I ordered. "You don't carry anything out with you."

His fingers worked with the buckle, dragged the belt from under his clothes, let it fall on the floor. It was padded fat.

Still holding his neck, I took him upstairs, while the girl still sat frozen on the kitchen chair. It took a stiff hooker of whisky and a lot of words to thaw her into understanding that she was going out with the old man and that she wasn't to say a word to anybody, especially not to the police.

"Where's Reddy?" she asked when color had come back into her face—which had even at the worst never lost its niceness—and thoughts to her head.

I told her he was all right, and promised her he would be in a hospital before the morning was over. She didn't ask anything else. I shooed her upstairs for her hat and coat, went with the old man while he got his hat, and then put the pair of them in the front ground-floor room.

"Stay here till I come for you," I said, and I locked the door and pocketed the key when I went out.

Chapter Fifteen

Flag of Truce

THE FRONT DOOR and the front window on the ground floor had been planked and braced like the rear ones. I didn't like to risk opening them, even though it was fairly light by now.

So I went upstairs, fashioned a flag of truce out of a pillow slip and a bed slat, hung it out a window, waited until a heavy voice said, "All right, speak your piece," and then I showed myself and told the police I'd let them in.

It took five minutes' work with a hatchet to pry the front door loose. The chief of police, the captain of detectives, and half the force were waiting on the front steps and pavement when I got the door open.

I took them to the cellar and turned Big Flora, Pogy and Red O'Leary over to them, with the money. Flora and Pogy were awake, but not talking.

While the dignitaries were crowded around the spoils I went upstairs. The house was full of police sleuths. I swapped greetings with them as I went through to the room where I had left Nancy Regan and the old gink Lieutenant Duff was trying the locked door, whil O'Gar and Hunt stood behind him.

I grinned at Duff and gave him the key.

He opened the door, looked at the old man and th girl—mostly at her—and then at me. They were standing in the center of the room. The old man's faded eye were miserably worried, the girl's blue ones were darkl anxious. Anxiety didn't ruin her looks a bit.

"If that's yours I don't blame you for locking it up," O'Gar muttered in my ear.

"You can run along now," I told the two in the room "Get all the sleep you need before you report for duty again."

They nodded and went out of the house.

"That's how your Agency evens up?" Duff said. "The she-employees make up in looks for the ugliness of the he's."

Dick Foley came into the hall.

"How's your end?" I asked.

"Finis. The Angel led me to Vance. He led here. I led the bulls here. They got him—got her."

Two shots crashed in the street.

We went to the door and saw excitement in a police car down the street. We went down there. Bluepoint Vance, handcuffs on his wrists, was writhing half on the seat, half on the floor.

"We were holding him here in the car, Houston and me," a hard-mouthed plain-clothes man explained to Duff. "He made a break, grabbed Houston's gat with both hands. I had to drill him—twice. The cap'll raise hell! He specially wanted him kept here to put up against the others. But God knows I wouldn't of shot him if it hadn't been him or Houston!"

Duff called the plain-clothes man a damned clumsy mick as they lifted Vance up on the seat. Bluepoint's tortured eyes focused on me.

"I—know—you?" he asked painfully. "Continental—New—York?"

"Yes," I said.

"Couldn't—place—you—Larrouy's—with—Red?"

"Yeah," I told him. "Got Red, Flora, Pogy and the cush."

"But—not—Papa—dop—oul—os."

"Papa does what?" I asked impatiently, a shiver along my spine.

He pulled himself up on the seat.

"Papadopoulos," he repeated, with an agonizing summoning of the little strength left in him. "I tried—shoot him—saw him—walk 'way—with girl—bull—too damn quick—wish . . ."

His words ran out. He shuddered. Death wasn't a sixteenth of an inch behind his eyes.

A white-coated intern tried to get past me into the car. I pushed him out of the way and leaned in taking Vance by the shoulders. The back of my neck was ice. My stomach was empty.

"Listen, Bluepoint," I yelled in his face. "Papadopoulos? Little old man? Brains of the push?"

"Yes," Vance said, and the last live blood in him came out with the word.

I let him drop back on the seat and walked away.

Of course! How had I missed it? The little old scoundrel—if he hadn't for all his scariness been the works, how could he have so neatly turned the others over to me one at a time? They had been absolutely cornered. It was be killed fighting, or surrender and be hanged. They had no other way out. The police had Vance, who could and would tell them that the little buzzard was the headman—there wasn't even a chance for him beating the courts with his age, his weakness and his mask of being driven around by the others.

And there I had been—with no choice but to accept his offer. Otherwise lights out for me. I had been putty in his hands; his accomplices had been putty. He had slipped the cross over on them as they had helped him slip it over on the others—and I had sent him safely away.

Now I could turn the city upside down for him—my promise had been only to get him out of the house—but . . .

What a life!

Part Two

THE LITTLE OLD MAN

Chapter One

$106,000 REWARD

"I'M TOM-TOM CAREY," he said, drawling the words.

I nodded at the chair beside my desk and weighed him in while he moved to it. Tall, wide-shouldered, thick-chested, thin-bellied, he would add up to, say, a hundred and ninety pounds. His swarthy face was hard as a fist, but there was nothing ill-humored in it. It was the face of a man of forty-something who lived life raw and thrived on it. His blue clothes were good and he wore them well.

In the chair, he twisted brown paper around a charge of Bull Durham and finished introducing himself:

"I'm Paddy the Mex's brother."

I thought maybe he was telling the truth. Paddy had been like this fellow in coloring and manner.

"That would make your real name Carrera," I suggested.

"Yes," he was lighting his cigarette. "Alfredo Estanislao Cristobal Carrera, if you want all the details."

I asked him how to spell Estanislao, wrote the name down on a slip of paper, adding *alias Tom-Tom Carey,* rang for Tommy Howd, and told him to have the file clerk see if we had anything on it.

"While your people are opening graves I'll tell you why I'm here," the swarthy man drawled through smoke when Tommy had gone away with the paper.

"Tough—Paddy being knocked off like that," I said.

"He was too damned trusting to live long," his brother explained. "This is the kind of hombre he was—the last time I saw him was four years ago, here in San Francisco. I'd come in from an expedition down to—never mind where. Anyway I was flat. Instead of pearls all I'd got out of the trip was a bullet-crease over my hip. Paddy was dirty with fifteen thousand or so he'd just nicked somebody for. The afternoon I saw him he had a date that he was leery of toting so much money to. So he gives me the fifteen thousand to hold for him till that night."

Tom-Tom Carey blew out smoke and smiled softly past me at a memory.

"That's the kind of hombre he was," he went on.

"He'd trust even his own brother. I went to Sacramento that afternoon and caught a train East. A girl in Pittsburgh helped me spend the fifteen thousand. Her name was Laurel. She liked rye whisky with milk for a chaser. I used to drink it with her till I was all curdled inside, and I've never had any appetite for *schmierkäse* since. So there's a hundred thousand dollars reward on this Papadopoulos, is there?"

"And six. The insurance companies put up a hundred thousand, the bankers' association five, and the city a thousand."

Tom-Tom Carey chucked the remains of his cigarette in the cuspidor and began to assemble another one.

"Suppose I hand him to you?" he asked. "How many ways will the money have to go?"

"None of it will stop here," I assured him. "The Continental Detective Agency doesn't touch reward money—and won't let its hired men. If any of the police are in on the pinch, they'll want a share."

"But if they aren't, it's all mine?"

"If you turn him in without help, or without any help except ours."

"I'll do that." The words were casual. "So much for the arrest. Now for the conviction part. If you get him, are you sure you can nail him to the cross?"

"I ought to be, but he'll have to go up against a jury—

and that means anything can happen."

The muscular brown hand holding the brown cigarette made a careless gesture.

"Then maybe I'd better get a confession out of him before I drag him in," he said off-hand.

"It would be safer that way," I agreed. "You ought to let that holster down an inch or two. It brings the gun-butt too high. The bulge shows when you sit down."

"Uh-huh. You mean the one on the left shoulder. I took it away from a fellow after I lost mine. Strap's too short. I'll get another one this afternoon."

Tommy came in with a folder labeled, *Carey, Tom-Tom, 1361-C.* It held some newspaper clippings, the oldest dated ten years back, the youngest eight months. I read them through, passing each one to the swarthy man as I finished it. Tom-Tom Carey was written down in them as soldier of fortune, gunrunner, seal poacher, smuggler, and pirate. But it was all alleged, supposed and suspected. He had been captured variously but never convicted of anything.

"They don't treat me right," he complained placidly when we were through reading. "For instance, stealing that Chinese gunboat wasn't my fault. I was forced to do it—I was the one that was double-crossed. After they'd got the stuff aboard they wouldn't pay for it. I couldn't unload it. I couldn't do anything but take gunboat and all. The insurance companies must want this Papadopoulos plenty to hang a hundred thousand on him."

"Cheap enough if it lands him," I said. "Maybe he's not all the newspapers picture him as, but he's more than a handful. He gathered a whole damned army of strong-arm men here, took over a block in the center of the financial district, looted the two biggest banks in the city, fought off the whole police department, made his getaway, ditched the army, used some of his lieutenants to bump off some more of them—that's where your brother Paddy got his—then, with the help of Pogy Reeve, Big Flora Brace and Red O'Leary, wiped out the rest of his lieutenants. And remember, these lieutenants weren't schoolboys—they were slick grifters like Blue-point Vance and the Shivering Kid and Darby M'Laughlin—birds who knew their what's what."

"Uh-huh." Carey was unimpressed. "But it was a bust just the same. You got all the loot back, and he just managed to get away himself."

"A bad break for him," I explained. "Red O'Leary broke out with a complication of love and vanity. You can't chalk that against Papadopoulos. Don't get the idea he's half-smart. He's dangerous, and I don't blame the insurance companies for thinking they'll sleep better if they're sure he's not out where he can frame some more tricks against their policy-holding banks."

"Don't know much about this Papadopoulos, do you?"

"No." I told the truth. "And nobody does. The hundred thousand offer made rats out of half the crooks in the country. They're as hot after him as we—not only because of the reward but because of his wholesale double-crossing. And they know just as little about him as we do—that he's had his fingers in a dozen or more jobs, that he was the brains behind Bluepoint Vance's bond tricks, and that his enemies have a habit of dying young. But nobody knows where he came from, or where he lives when he's home. Don't think I'm touting him as a Napoleon or a Sunday-supplement master mind—but he's a shifty, tricky old boy. As you say, I don't know much about him—but there are lots of people I don't know much about."

Tom-Tom Carey nodded to show he understood the last part and began making his third cigarette.

"I was in Nogales when Angel Grace Cardigan got word to me that Paddy had been done in," he said. "That was nearly a month ago. She seemed to think I'd romp up here pronto—but it was no skin off my face. I let it sleep. But last week I read in a newspaper about all this reward money being posted on the hombre she blamed for Paddy's rub-out. That made it different—a hundred thousand dollars different. So I shipped up here, talked to her, and then came in to make sure there'll be nothing between me and the blood money when I put the loop on this Papadoodle."

"Angel Grace sent you to me?" I inquired.

"Uh-huh—only she don't know it. She dragged you into the story—said you were a friend of Paddy's, a good guy for a sleuth, and hungry as hell for this Papadoodle. So I thought you'd be the gent for me to see."

"When did you leave Nogales?"

"Tuesday—last week."

"That," I said, prodding my memory, "was the day after Newhall was killed across the border."

The swarthy man nodded. Nothing changed in his face.

"How far from Nogales was that?" I asked.

"He was gunned down near Oquitoa—that's somewhere around sixty miles southwest of Nogales. You interested?"

"No—except I was wondering about your leaving the place where he was killed the day after he was killed, and coming up where he had lived. Did you know him?"

"He was pointed out to me in Nogales as a San Francisco millionaire going with a party to look at some mining property in Mexico. I was figuring on maybe selling him something later, but the Mexican patriots got him before I did."

"And so you came north?"

"Uh-huh. The hubbub kind of spoiled things for me. I had a nice little business in—call it supplies—to and fro across the line. This Newhall killing turned the spotlight on that part of the country. So I thought I'd come up and collect that hundred thousand and give things a chance to settle down there. Honest, brother, I haven't killed a millionaire in weeks, if that's what's worrying you."

"That's good. Now, as I get it, you're counting on landing Papadopoulos. Angel Grace sent for you, thinking you'd run him down just to even up for Paddy's killing, but it's the money you want, so you figure on playing with me as well as the Angel. That right?"

"Check."

"You know what'll happen if she learns you're stringing along with me?"

"Uh-huh. She'll chuck a convulsion—kind of balmy on the subject of keeping clear of the police, isn't she?"

"She is—somebody told her something about honor among thieves once and she's never got over it. Her brother's doing a hitch up north now—Johnny the Plumber sold him out. Her man Paddy was mowed down by his pals. Did either of those things wake her up? Not a chance. She'd rather have Papadopoulos go free than join forces with us."

"That's all right," Tom-Tom Carey assured me. "She thinks I'm the loyal brother—Paddy couldn't have told her much about me—and I'll handle her. You having her shadowed?"

I said, "Yes—ever since she was turned loose. She was picked up the same day Flora and Pogy and Red were grabbed, but we hadn't anything on her except that she had been Paddy's ladylove, so I had her sprung. How much dope did you get out of her?"

"Descriptions of Papadoodle and Nancy Regan, and that's all. She don't know any more about them than I do. Where does this Regan girl fit in?"

"Hardly any, except that she might lead us to Papadopoulos. She was Red's girl. It was keeping a date with her that upset the game. When Papadopoulos wriggled out he took the girl with him. I don't know why. She wasn't in on the stick-ups."

Tom-Tom Carey finished making and lighting his fifth cigarette and stood up.

"Are we teamed?" he asked as he picked up his hat.

"If you turn in Papadopoulos I'll see that you get every nickel you're entitled to," I replied. "And I'll give you a clear field—I won't handicap you with too much of an attempt to keep my eyes on your actions."

He said that was fair enough, told me he was stopping at a hotel in Ellis Street, and went away.

Chapter Two

The Lisping Lawyer

Calling the late Taylor Newhall's office on the phone, I was told that if I wanted any information about his affairs I should try his country residence, some miles south of San Francisco. I tried it.

A ministerial voice that said it belonged to the butler told me that Newhall's attorney, Franklin Ellert, was the person I should see. I went over to Ellert's office.

He was a nervous, irritable old man with a lisp and eyes that stuck out with blood pressure.

"Is there any reason," I asked pointblank, "for supposing that Newhall's murder was anything more than a Mexican bandit outburst? Is it likely that he was killed purposely, and not resisting capture?"

Lawyers don't like to be questioned. This one sputtered and made faces at me and let his eyes stick out still further and, of course, didn't give me an answer.

"How? How?" he snapped disagreeably. "Exthplain your meaning, thir!"

He glared at me and then at the desk, pushing papers

around with excited hands, as if he were hunting for a police whistle. I told my story—told him about Tom-Tom Carey.

Ellert sputtered some more, demanded, "What the devil do you mean?" and made a complete jumble of the papers on his desk.

"I don't mean anything," I growled back. "I'm just telling you what was said."

"Yeth! Yeth! I know!" He stopped glaring at me and his voice was less peevish. "But there ith abtholutely no reathon for thuthpecting anything of the thort. None at all, thir, none at all!"

"Maybe you're right." I turned to the door. "But I'll poke into it a little anyway."

"Wait! Wait!" He scrambled out of his chair and ran around the desk to me. "I think you are mithtaken, but if you are going to invethtigate it I would like to know what you dithcover. Perhapth you'd better charge me with your regular fee for whatever ith done, and keep me informed of your progreth. Thatithfactory?"

I said it was, came back to his desk and began to question him.

There was, as the lawyer had said, nothing in Newhall's affairs to stir us up. The dead man was several times a millionaire, with most of his money in mines. He had inherited nearly half his money. There was no shady practice, no claim jumping, no trickery in his past, no enemies. He was a widower with one daughter. She had everything she wanted while he lived, and she and her father had been very fond of one another. He had gone to Mexico with a party of mining men from New York who expected to sell him some property there. They had been attacked by bandits, had driven them off, but Newhall and a geologist named Parker had been killed during the fight.

Back in the office, I wrote a telegram to our Los Angeles branch, asking that an operative be sent to Nogales to pry into Newhall's killing and Tom-Tom Carey's affairs. The clerk to whom I gave it to be coded and sent told me the Old Man wanted to see me. I went into his office and was introduced to a short, roly-poly man named Hook.

"Mr. Hook," the Old Man said, "is the proprietor of a restaurant in Sausalito. Last Monday he employed a waitress named Nelly Riley. She told him she had come from Los Angeles. Her description, as Mr. Hook gives it, is quite similar to the description you and Counihan have given of Nancy Regan. Isn't it?" he asked the fat man.

"Absolutely. It's exactly what I read in the papers. She's five feet five inches tall, about, and medium in size, and she's got blue eyes and brown hair, and she's around twenty-one or -two, and she's got looks, and the thing that counts most is she's high-hat as the devil—she don't think nothin's good enough for her. Why, when I tried to be a little sociable she told me to keep my 'dirty paws' to myself. And then I found out she didn't know hardly nothing about Los Angeles, though she claimed to have lived there two or three years. I bet you she's the girl, all right," and he went on talking about how much reward money he ought to get.

"Are you going back there now?" I asked him.

"Pretty soon. I got to stop and see about some dishes. Then I'm going back."

"This girl will be working?"

"Yes."

"Then we'll send a man over with you—one who knows Nancy Regan."

I called Jack Counihan in from the operatives' room and introduced him to Hook. They arranged to meet in half an hour at the ferry and Hook waddled out.

"This Nelly Riley won't be Nancy Regan," I said. "But we can't afford to pass up even a hundred-to-one chance."

I told Jack and the Old Man about Tom-Tom Carey and my visit to Ellert's office. The Old Man listened with his usual polite attentiveness. Young Counihan—only four months in the man-hunting business—listened with wide eyes.

"You'd better run along now and meet Hook," I said when I had finished, leaving the Old Man's office with Jack. "And if she should be Nancy Regan—grab her and hang on." We were out of the Old Man's hearing, so I added, "And for God's sake don't let your youthful gallantry lead you to a poke in the jaw this time."

The boy blushed, said, "Go to hell!" adjusted his necktie, and set off to meet Hook.

I had some reports to write. After I had finished them I put my feet on my desk, made cavities in a package of Fatimas, and thought about Tom-Tom Carey until six o'clock. Then I went down to the States for my abalone chowder and minute steak and home to change clothes before going out Sea Cliff way to sit in a poker game.

The telephone interrupted my dressing. Jack Counihan was on the other end.

"I'm in Sausalito. The girl wasn't Nancy, but I've got hold of something else. I'm not sure how to handle it. Can you come over?"

"Is it important enough to cut a poker game for?"

"Yes, it's—I think it's big." He was excited. "I wish you would come over. I really think it's a lead."

"Where are you?"

"At the ferry there. Not the Golden Gate, the other."

"All right. I'll catch the first boat."

Chapter Three

The Shack

An hour later I walked off the boat in Sausalito. Jack Counihan pushed through the crowd and began talking:

"Coming down here on my way back—"

"Hold it till we get out of the mob," I advised him. "It must be tremendous—the eastern point of your collar is bent."

He mechanically repaired this defect in his otherwise immaculate costuming while we walked to the street, but he was too intent on whatever was on his mind to smile.

"Up this way," he said, guiding me around a corner. "Hook's lunchroom is on the corner. You can take a look at the girl if you like. She's of the same size and complexion as Nancy Regan, but that is all. She's a tough little job who probably was fired for dropping her chewing gum in the soup the last place she worked."

"All right. That let's her out. Now what's on your mind?"

"After I saw her I started back to the ferry. A boat came in while I was still a couple of blocks away. Two men who must have come in on it came up the street. They were Greeks, rather young, tough, though ordinarily I shouldn't have paid much attention to them. But, since Papadopoulos is a Greek, we have been interested in them, of course, so I looked at these chaps. They were arguing about something as they walked, not talking loud, but scowling at one another. As they passed me the chap on the gutter side said to the other, 'I tell him it's been twenty-nine days.'

"Twenty-nine days. I counted back and it's just twenty-nine days since we started hunting for Papadopoulos. He is a Greek and these chaps were Greeks. When I had finished counting I turned around and began to follow them. They took me all the way through the town and up a hill on the fringe. They went to a little cottage—it couldn't have more than three rooms—set back in a clearing in the woods by itself. There was a 'For Sale' sign on it, and no curtains in the windows, no sign of occupancy—but on the ground behind the back door there was a wet place, as if a bucket or pan of water had been thrown out.

"I stayed in the bushes until it got a little darker. Then I went closer. I could hear people inside, but I couldn't see anything through the windows. They're boarded up. After a while the two chaps I had followed came out, saying something in a language I couldn't understand to whoever was in the cottage. The cottage door stayed open until the two men had gone out of sight down the path—so I couldn't have followed them without being seen by whoever was at the door.

"Then the door was closed and I could hear people moving around inside—or perhaps only one person—and could smell cooking, and some smoke came out of the chimney. I waited and waited and nothing more happened and I thought I had better get in touch with you."

"Sounds interesting," I agreed.

We were passing under a street light. Jack stopped me with a hand on my arm and fished something out of his overcoat pocket.

"Look!" He held it out to me.

A charred piece of blue cloth. It could have been the remains of a woman's hat that had been three-quarters burned. I looked at it under the street light and then used my flashlight to examine it more closely.

"I picked it up behind the cottage while I was nosing around," Jack said, "and—"

"And Nancy Regan wore a hat of that shade the night she and Papadopoulos vanished," I finished for him. "On to the cottage."

We left the street lights behind, climbed the hill, dipped down into a little valley, turned into a winding sandy path, left that to cut across sod between trees to a dirt road, trod half a mile of that, and then Jack led the way along a narrow path that wound through a black tangle of bushes and small trees.

I hoped he knew where he was going.

"Almost there," he whispered to me.

A man jumped out of the bushes and took me by the neck.

My hands were in my overcoat pockets—one holding the flashlight, the other my gun.

I pushed the muzzle of the pocketed gun toward the man—pulled the trigger.

The shot ruined seventy-five dollars' worth of overcoat for me. But it took the man away from my neck.

That was lucky. Another man was on my back.

I tried to twist away from him—didn't altogether make it—felt the edge of a knife along my spine.

That wasn't so lucky—but it was better than getting the point.

I butted back at his face—missed—kept twisting and squirming while I brought my hands out of my pockets and clawed at him.

The blade of his knife came flat against my cheek. I caught the hand that held it and let myself go—down backward—him under.

He said, "Uh!"

I rolled over, got hands and knees on the ground, was grazed by a fist, scrambled up.

Fingers dragged at my ankle.

My behavior was ungentlemanly. I kicked the fingers away, found the man's body—kicked it twice, hard.

Jack's voice whispered my name. I couldn't see him in the blackness, nor could I see the man I had shot.

"All right here," I told Jack. "How did you come out?"

"Top-hole. Is that all of it?"

"Don't know, but I'm going to risk a peek at what I've got."

Tilting my flashlight down at the man under my foot, I snapped it on. A thin blond man, his face blood-smeared, his pink-rimmed eyes jerking as he tried to play possum in the glare.

"Come out of it!" I ordered.

A heavy gun went off back in the bush—another lighter one. The bullets ripped through the foliage.

I switched off the light, bent to the man on the ground, knocked him on the top of the head with my gun.

"Crouch down low," I whispered to Jack.

The smaller gun snapped again, twice. It was ahead, to the left.

I put my mouth to Jack's ear.

"We're going to that damned cottage whether anybody likes it or no. Keep low and don't do any shooting unless you can see what you're shooting at. Go ahead."

Bending as close to the ground as I could, I followed Jack up the path. The position stretched the slash in my back—a scalding pain from between my shoulders almost to my waist. I could feel blood trickling down over my hips—or thought I could.

The going was too dark for stealthiness. Things crackled under our feet, rustled against our shoulders. Our friends in the bush used their guns. Luckily, the sound of twigs breaking and leaves rustling in pitch blackness isn't the best of targets. Bullets zipped here and there, but we didn't stop any of them. Neither did we shoot back.

We halted where the end of the bush left the night a weaker gray.

"That's it," Jack said about a square shape ahead.

"On the jump," I grunted and lit out for the dark cottage.

Jack's long slim legs kept him easily at my side as we raced across the clearing.

A man-shape oozed from behind the blot of the building and his gun began to blink at us. The shots came so close together that they sounded like one long stuttering bang.

Pulling the youngster with me I flopped, flat to the ground except where a ragged-edged empty tin-can held my face up.

From the other side of the building another gun coughed. From a tree-stem to the right, a third.

Jack and I began to burn powder back at them.

A bullet kicked my mouth full of dirt and pebbles. I spit mud and cautioned Jack:

"You're shooting too high. Hold it low and pull easy."

A hump showed in the house's dark profile. I sent a bullet at it.

A man's voice yelled, "Ow—ooh!" and then, lower but very bitter, "Oh, damn you—damn you!"

For a warm couple of seconds bullets spattered all around us. Then there was not a sound to spoil the night's quietness.

When the silence had lasted five minutes, I got myself up on hands and knees and began to move forward, Jack following. The ground wasn't made for that sort of work. Ten feet of it was enough. We stood up and walked the rest of the way to the building.

"Wait," I whispered, and, leaving Jack at one corner of the building, I circled it, seeing nobody, hearing nothing but the sounds I made.

We tried the front door. It was locked but rickety.

Bumping it open with my shoulder, I went indoors—flashlight and gun in my fists.

The shack was empty.

Nobody—no furnishings, no traces of either in the two bare rooms—nothing but bare wooden walls, bare floor, bare ceiling, with a stove-pipe connected to nothing through it.

Jack and I stood in the middle of the floor, looked at the emptiness, and cursed the dump from back door to front for being empty. We hadn't quite finished when feet sounded outside, a white light beamed on the open doorway, and a cracked voice said:

"Hey! You can come out one at a time—kind of easy like!"

"Who says so?" I asked, snapping off the flashlight, moving over close to a side wall.

"A whole goldurned flock of deputy sheriffs," the voice answered.

"Couldn't you push one of 'em in and let us get a look at him?" I asked. "I've been choked and carved and shot at tonight until I haven't got much faith left in anybody's word."

A lanky, knock-kneed man with a thin leathery face appeared in the doorway. He showed me a buzzer, I fished out my credentials, and the other deputies came in. There were three of them in all.

"We were driving down the road bound for a little job near the point when we heard the shooting," the lanky one explained. "What's up?"

I told him.

"This shack's been empty a long while," he said when I had finished. "Anybody could have camped in it easy enough. Think it was that Papadopoulos, huh? We'll kind of look around for him and his friends—especial since there's that nice reward money."

We searched the woods and found nobody. The man I had knocked down and the man I had shot were both gone.

Jack and I rode back to Sausalito with the deputies. I hunted up a doctor there and had my back bandaged. He said the cut was long but shallow. Then we returned to San Francisco and separated in the direction of our homes.

And thus ended the day's doings.

Chapter Four

HARBOR HOSPITAL

HERE IS SOMETHING that happened next morning. I didn't see it. I heard about it a little before noon and read about it in the papers that afternoon. I didn't know then that I had any personal interest in it, but later I did —so I'll put it in here where it happened.

At ten o'clock that morning, into busy Market Street staggered a man who was naked from the top of his battered head to the soles of his blood-stained feet. From his bare chest and sides and back, little ribbons of flesh hung down, dripping blood. His left arm was broken in two places. The left side of his bald head was smashed in.

An hour later he died in the emergency hospital—without having said a word to anyone, with the same vacant, distant look in his eyes.

The police easily ran back the trail of blood drops. They ended with a red smear in an alley beside a small hotel just off Market Street. In the hotel, the police found the room from which the man had jumped, fallen, or been thrown. The bed was soggy with blood. On it were torn and twisted sheets that had been knotted and used rope-wise. There was also a towel that had been used as a gag.

The evidence read that the naked man had been gagged, trussed up and worked on with a knife. The doctors said the ribbons of flesh had been cut loose, not torn or clawed. After the knife-user had gone away, the naked man had worked free of his bonds, and, probably crazed by pain, had either jumped or fallen out of the window. The fall had crushed his skull and broken his arm, but he had managed to walk a block and a half in that condition.

The hotel management said the man had been there two days. He was registered as H. F. Barrows, City. He had a black gladstone bag in which, besides clothes, shaving implements and so on, the police found a box of .38 cartridges, a black handkerchief with eyeholes cut in it, four skeleton keys, a small jimmy, and a quantity of morphine, with a needle and the rest of the kit. Elsewhere in the room they found the rest of his clothes, a .38 revolver and two quarts of liquor. They didn't find a cent.

The supposition was that Barrows had been a burglar, and that he had been tied up, tortured and robbed, probably by pals, between eight and nine that morning.

Nobody knew anything about him. Nobody had seen his visitor or visitors. The room next to his on the left was unoccupied. The occupant of the room on the other side had left for his work in a furniture factory before seven o'clock.

While this was happening I was at the office, sitting forward in my chair to spare my back, reading reports, all of which told how operatives attached to various Continental Detective Agency branches had continued to fail to turn up any indications of the past, present, or future whereabouts of Papadopoulos and Nancy Regan.

There was nothing novel about these reports—I had been reading similar ones for three weeks.

The Old Man and I went out to luncheon together, and I told him about the previous night's adventures in Sausalito while we ate. His grandfatherly face was as attentive as always, and his smile as politely interested, but when I was half through my story he turned his mild blue eyes from my face to his salad and he stared at his salad until I had finished talking. Then, still not looking up, he said he was sorry I had been cut. I thanked him and we ate a while.

Finally he looked at me. The mildness and courtesy he habitually wore over his cold-bloodedness were in face and eyes and voice as he said:

"This first indication that Papadopoulos is still alive

came immediately after Tom-Tom Carey's arrival."

It was my turn to shift my eyes.

I looked at the roll I was breaking while I said, "Yes."

That afternoon a phone call came in from a woman out in the Mission who had seen some highly mysterious happenings and was sure they had something to do with the well-advertised bank robberies. So I went out to see her and spent most of the afternoon learning that half of her happenings were imaginary and the other half were the efforts of a jealous wife to get the low-down on her husband.

It was nearly six o'clock when I returned to the Agency. A few minutes later Dick Foley called me on the phone. His teeth were chattering so I could hardly get the words.

"C-c-canyoug-g-get-t-townt-t-tooth ar-r-r-rbr-spittle?"

"What?" I asked, and he said the same thing again, or worse.

But by this time I had guessed that he was asking me if I could get down to the Harbor Hospital.

I told him I could in ten minutes, and with the help of a taxi I did.

Chapter Five

Her Side of the Fence

The little Canadian operative met me at the hospital door. His clothes and hair were dripping wet, but he had had a shot of whisky and his teeth had stopped chattering.

"Damned fool jumped in bay!" he barked as if it were my fault.

"Angel Grace?"

"Who else was I shadowing? Got on Oakland ferry. Moved off by self by rail. Thought she was going to throw something over. Kept eye on her. Bingo! She jumps." Dick sneezed. "I was goofy enough to jump after her. Held her up. Were fished out. In there," nodding his wet head toward the interior of the hospital.

"What happened before she took the ferry?"

"Nothing. Been in joint all day. Straight out to ferry."

"How about yesterday?"

"Apartment all day. Out at night with man. Roadhouse. Home at four. Bad break. Couldn't tail him off."

"What did he look like?"

The man Dick described was Tom-Tom Carey.

"Good," I said. "You'd better beat it home for a hot bath and some dry rags."

I went in to see the near-suicide.

She was lying on her back on a cot, staring at the ceiling. Her face was pale, but it always was, and her green eyes were no more sullen than usual. Except that her short hair was dark with dampness she didn't look as if anything out of the ordinary had happened.

"You think of the funniest things to do," I said when I was beside the bed.

She jumped and her face jerked around to me, startled. Then she recognized me and smiled—a smile that brought into her face the attractiveness that habitual sullenness kept out.

"You have to keep in practice—sneaking up on people?" she asked. "Who told you I was here?"

"Everybody knows it. Your pictures are all over the front pages of the newspapers, with your life history and what you said to the Prince of Wales."

She stopped smiling and looked steadily at me.

"I got it!" she exclaimed after a few seconds. "That runt who came in after me was one of your ops—tailing me. Wasn't he?"

"I didn't know anybody had to go in after you," I answered. "I thought you came ashore after you had finished your swim. Didn't you want to land?"

She wouldn't smile. Her eyes began to look at something horrible.

"Oh! Why didn't they let me alone?" she wailed, shuddering. "It's a rotten thing, living."

I sat down on a small chair beside the white bed and patted the lump her shoulder made in the sheets.

"What was it?" I was surprised at the fatherly tone I achieved. "What did you want to die for, Angel?"

Words that wanted to be said were shiny in her eyes, tugged at muscles in her face, shaped her lips—but that was all. The words she said came out listlessly, but with a reluctant sort of finality. They were:

"No. You're law. I'm thief. I'm staying on my side of the fence. Nobody can say—"

"All right! All right!" I surrendered. "But for God's sake don't make me listen to another of those ethical arguments. Is there anything I can do for you?"

"Thanks, no."

"There's nothing you want to tell me?"

She shook her head.

"You're all right now?"

"Yes. I was being shadowed, wasn't I? Or you wouldn't have known about it so soon."

"I'm a detective—I know everything. Be a good girl."

From the hospital I went up to the Hall of Justice, to

the police detective bureau. Lieutenant Duff was holding down the captain's desk. I told him about the Angel's dive.

"Got any idea what she was up to?" he wanted to know when I had finished.

"She's too far off center to figure. I want her vagged."

"Yeah? I thought you wanted her loose so you could catch her."

"That's about played out now. I'd like to try throwing her in the can for thirty days. Big Flora is in waiting trial. The Angel knows Flora was one of the troupe that rubbed out her Paddy. Maybe Flora don't know the Angel. Let's see what will come of mixing the two babies for a month."

"Can do," Duff agreed. "This Angel's got no visible means of support and it's a cinch she's got no business running around jumping in people's bays. I'll put the word through."

From the Hall of Justice I went up to the Ellis Street hotel at which Tom-Tom Carey had told me he was registered. He was out.

I left word that I would be back in an hour, and used that hour to eat. When I returned to the hotel the tall swarthy man was sitting in the lobby. He took me up to his room and set out gin, orange juice and cigars.

"Seen Angel Grace?" I asked.

"Yes, last night. We did the dumps."

"Seen her today?"

"No."

"She jumped in the bay this afternoon."

"The hell she did." He seemed moderately surprised. "And then?"

"She was fished out. She's O. K."

The shadow in his eyes could have been some slight disappointment.

"She's a funny sort of kid," he remarked. "I wouldn't say Paddy didn't show good taste when he picked her, but she's a queer one!"

"How's the Papadopoulos hunt progressing?"

"It is. But you oughtn't have split on your word. You half-way promised you wouldn't have me shadowed."

"I'm not the big boss," I apologized. "Sometimes what I want don't fit in with what the headman wants. This shouldn't bother you much—you can shake him, can't you?"

"Uh-huh. That's what I've been doing. But it's a damned nuisance jumping in and out of taxis and back doors."

We talked and drank a few minutes longer, and then I left Carey's room and hotel, and went to a drugstore telephone booth, where I called Dick Foley's home, and gave Dick the swarthy man's description and address.

"I don't want you to tail Carey, Dick. I want you to find out who is trying to tail him—and that shadower is the bird you're to stick to. The morning will be time enough to start—get yourself dried out."

And that was the end of that day.

Chapter Six

R. I. P.

I WOKE to a disagreeable rainy morning. Maybe it was the weather, maybe I'd been too frisky the day before, anyway the slit in my back was like a foot-long boil.

I phoned Dr. Canova, who lived on the floor below me, and had him look at the cut before he left for his downtown office. He rebandaged it and told me to take life easy for a couple of days. It felt better after he had fooled with it, but I phoned the Agency and told the Old Man that unless something exciting broke I was going to stay on sick-call all day.

I spent the day propped up in front of the gas-log, reading, and smoking cigarettes that wouldn't burn right on account of the weather. That night I used the phone to organize a poker game, in which I got very little action one way or the other. In the end I was fifteen dollars ahead, which was just about five dollars less than enough to pay for the booze my guests had drunk on me.

My back was better the following day, and so was

the day. I went down to the Agency. There was a memorandum on my desk saying Duff had phoned that Angel Grace Cardigan had been vagged—thirty days in the city prison. There was a familiar pile of reports from various branches on their operatives' inability to pick up anything on Papadopoulos and Nancy Regan. I was running through these when Dick Foley came in.

"Made him," he reported. "Thirty or thirty-two. Five, six. Hundred, thirty. Sandy hair, complexion. Blue eye. Thin face, some skin off. Rat. Lives dump in Seventh Street."

"What did he do?"

"Tailed Carey one block. Carey shook him. Hunted for Carey till two in morning. Didn't find him. Went home. Take him again?"

"Go up to his flophouse and find out who he is."

The little Canadian was gone half an hour.

"Sam Arlie," he said when he returned. "Been there six months. Supposed to be barber—when he's working —if ever."

"I've got two guesses about this Arlie," I told Dick. "The first is that he's the gink who carved me in Sausalito the other night. The second is that something's going to happen to him."

It was against Dick's rules to waste words, so he said nothing.

I called Tom-Tom Carey's hotel and got the swarthy man on the wire.

"Come over," I invited him. "I've got some news for you."

"As soon as I'm dressed and breakfasted," he promised.

"When Carey leaves here you're to go along behind him," I told Dick after I had hung up. "If Arlie connects with him now, maybe there'll be something doing. Try to see it."

Then I phoned the detective bureau and made a date with Sergeant Hunt to visit Angel Grace Cardigan's apartment. After that I busied myself with paper work until Tommy came in to announce the swarthy man from Nogales.

"The jobbie who's tailing you," I informed him when he had sat down and begun work on a cigarette, "is a barber named Arlie," and I told him where Arlie lived.

"Yes. A slim-faced, sandy lad?"

I gave him the description Dick had given me.

"That's the hombre," Tom-Tom Carey said. "Know anything else about him?"

"No."

"You had Angel Grace vagged."

It was neither an accusation nor a question, so I didn't answer it.

"It's just as well," the tall man went on. "I'd have had to send her away. She was bound to gum things with her foolishness when I got ready to swing the loop."

"That'll be soon?"

"That all depends on how it happens." He stood up, yawned and shook his wide shoulders. "But nobody would starve to death if they decided not to eat any more till I'd got him. I oughtn't have accused you of having me shadowed."

"It didn't spoil my day."

Tom-Tom Carey said, "So long," and sauntered out.

I rode down to the Hall of Justice, picked up Hunt, and we went to the Bush Street apartment house in which Angel Grace Cardigan had lived. The manager—a highly scented fat woman with a hard mouth and soft eyes—already knew her tenant was in the cooler. She willingly took us up to the girl's rooms.

The Angel wasn't a good housekeeper. Things were clean enough, but upset. The kitchen sink was full of dirty dishes. The folding bed was worse than loosely made up. Clothes and odds and ends of feminine equipment hung over everything from bathroom to kitchen.

We got rid of the landlady and raked the place over thoroughly. We came away knowing all there was to know about the girl's wardrobe, and a lot about her personal habits. But we didn't find anything pointing

Papadopoulosward.

No report came in on the Carey-Arlie combination that afternoon or evening, though I expected to hear from Dick every minute.

At three o'clock in the morning my bedside phone took my ear out of the pillows. The voice that came over the wire was the Canadian op's.

"Exit Arlie," he said.

"R. I. P.?"

"Yep."

"How?"

"Lead."

"Our lad's?"

"Yep."

"Keep till morning?"

"Yep."

"See you at the office," and I went back to sleep.

Chapter Seven

A Clean Sneak

When I arrived at the Agency at nine o'clock, one of the clerks had just finished decoding a night letter from the Los Angeles operative who had been sent over to Nogales. It was a long telegram, and meaty.

It said that Tom-Tom Carey was well known along the border. For some six months he had been engaged in over-the-line traffic—guns going south, booze, and probably dope and immigrants, coming north. Just before leaving there the previous week he had made inquiries concerning one Hank Barrows. This Hank Barrows' description fit the H. F. Barrows who had been cut into ribbons, who had fallen out the hotel window and died.

The Los Angeles operative hadn't been able to get much of a line on Barrows, except that he hailed from San Francisco, had been on the border only a few days, and had apparently returned to San Francisco. The operative had turned up nothing new on the Newhall killing—the signs still read that he had been killed resisting capture by Mexican patriots.

Dick Foley came into my office while I was reading the news. When I had finished he gave me his contribution to the history of Tom-Tom Carey.

"Tailed him out of here. To hotel. Arlie on corner. Eight o'clock, Carey out. Garage. Hire car without driver. Back hotel. Checked out. Two bags. Out through park. Arlie after him in flivver. My boat after Arlie. Down boulevard. Off cross-road. Dark. Lonely. Arlie steps on gas. Closes in. Bang! Carey stops. Two guns going. Exit Arlie. Carey back to city. Hotel Marquis. Registers George F. Danby, San Diego. Room 622."

"Did Tom-Tom frisk Arlie after he dropped him?"

"No. Didn't touch him."

"So? Take Mickey Linehan with you. Don't let Carey get out of your sight. I'll get somebody up to relieve you and Mickey late tonight, if I can, but he's got to be shadowed twenty-four hours a day until—"

I didn't know what came after that so I stopped talking.

I took Dick's story into the Old Man's office and told it to him, winding up:

"Arlie shot first, according to Foley, so Carey gets a self-defense on it, but we're getting action at last and I don't want to do anything to slow it up. So I'd like to keep what we know about this shooting quiet for a couple of days. It won't increase our friendship any with the county sheriff if he finds out what we're doing, but I think it's worth it."

"If you wish," the Old Man agreed, reaching for his ringing phone.

He spoke into the instrument and passed it on to me. Detective-sergeant Hunt was talking:

"Flora Brace and Grace Cardigan crushed out just before daylight. The chances are they—"

I wasn't in a humor for details.

"A clean sneak?" I asked.

"Not a lead on 'em so far, but—"

"I'll get the details when I see you. Thanks," and I hung up.

"Angel Grace and Big Flora have escaped from the city prison," I passed the news on to the Old Man.

He smiled courteously, as if at something that didn't especially concern him.

"You were congratulating yourself on getting action," he murmured.

I turned my scowl to a grin, mumbled, "Well, maybe," went back to my office and telephoned Franklin Ellert. The lisping attorney said he would be glad to see me, so I went over to his office.

"And now, what progreth have you made?" he asked eagerly when I was seated beside his desk.

"Some. A man named Barrows was also in Nogales

when Newhall was killed, and also came to San Francisco right after. Carey followed Barrows up here. Did you read about the man found walking the streets naked, all cut up?"

"Yeth."

"That was Barrows. Then another man comes into the game—a barber named Arlie. He was spying on Carey. Last night, in a lonely road south of here, Arlie shot at Carey. Carey killed him."

The old lawyer's eyes came out another inch.

"What road?" he gasped.

"You want the exact location?"

"Yeth!"

I pulled his phone over, called the Agency, had Dick's report read to me, gave the attorney the information he wanted.

It had an effect on him. He hopped out of his chair. Sweat was shiny along the ridges wrinkles made in his face.

"Mith Newhall ith down there alone! That plathe ith only half a mile from her houth!"

I frowned and beat my brains together, but I couldn't make anything out of it.

"Suppose I put a man down there to look after her?" I suggested.

"Exthellent!" His worried face cleared until there

weren't more than fifty or sixty wrinkles in it. "The would prefer to thtay there during her firth grief over her fatherth death. You will thend a capable man?"

"The Rock of Gibraltar is a leaf in the breeze beside him. Give me a note for him to take down. Andrew MacElroy is his name."

While the lawyer scribbled the note I used his phone again to call the Agency, to tell the operator to get hold of Andy and tell him I wanted him. I ate lunch before I returned to the Agency. Andy was waiting when I got there.

Andy MacElroy was a big boulder of a man—not very tall, but thick and hard of head and body. A glum, grim man with no more imagination than an adding machine. I'm not even sure he could read. But I was sure that when Andy was told to do something, he did it and nothing else. He didn't know enough not to.

I gave him the lawyer's note to Miss Newhall, told him where to go and what to do, and Miss Newhall's troubles were off my mind.

Three times that afternoon I heard from Dick Foley and Mickey Linehan. Tom-Tom Carey wasn't doing anything very exciting, though he had bought two boxes of .44 cartridges in a Market Street sporting goods establishment.

The afternoon papers carried photographs of Big

Flora Brace and Angel Grace Cardigan, with a story of their escape. The story was as far from the probable facts as newspaper stories generally are.

On another page was an account of the discovery of the dead barber in the lonely road. He had been shot in the head and in the chest, four times in all. The county officials' opinion was that he had been killed resisting a stick-up, and that the bandits had fled without robbing him.

At five o'clock Tommy Howd came to my door.

"That guy Carey wants to see you again," the freckle-faced boy said.

"Shoot him in."

The swarthy man sauntered in, said "Howdy," sat down, and made a brown cigarette.

"Got anything special on for tonight?" he asked when he was smoking.

"Nothing I can't put aside for something better. Giving a party?"

"Uh-huh. I had thought of it. A kind of surprise party on Papadoodle. Want to go along?"

It was my turn to say, "Uh-huh."

"I'll pick you up at eleven—Van Ness and Geary," he drawled. "But this has got to be a kind of tight party—just you and me—and him."

"No. There's one more who'll have to be in on it. I'll

bring him along."

"I don't like that." Tom-Tom Carey shook his head slowly, frowning amiably over his cigarette. "You sleuths oughtn't out-number me. It ought to be one and one."

"You won't be outnumbered," I explained. "This jobbie I'm bringing won't be on my side more than yours. And it'll pay you to keep as sharp an eye on him as I do—and to see he don't get behind either of us if we can help it."

"Then what do you want to lug him along for?"

"Wheels within wheels," I grinned.

The swarthy man frowned again, less amiably now.

"The hundred and six thousand reward money—I'm not figuring on sharing that with anybody."

"Right enough," I agreed. "Nobody I bring along will declare themselves in on it."

"I'll take your word for it." He stood up. "And we've got to watch this hombre, huh?"

"If we want everything to go all right."

"Suppose he gets in the way—cuts up on us. Can we put it to him, or do we just say, 'Naughty! Naughty!' "

"He'll have to take his own chances."

"Fair enough." His hard face was good-natured again as he moved toward the door. "Eleven o'clock at Van Ness and Geary."

Chapter Eight

The Girl in the Moonlight

I went back into the operatives' room, where Jack Counihan was slumped down in a chair reading a magazine.

"I hope you've thought up something for me to do," he greeted me. "I'm getting bedsores from sitting around."

"Patience, son, patience—that's what you've got to learn if you're ever going to be a detective. Why, when I was a child your age, just starting in with the Agency, I was lucky—"

"Don't start that," he begged. Then his good-looking young face got earnest. "I don't see why you keep me cooped up here. I'm the only one besides you who really got a good look at Nancy Regan. I should think you would have me out hunting for her."

"I told the Old Man the same thing," I sympathized. "But he is afraid to risk something happening to you. He says in all his fifty years of gumshoeing he's never seen such a handsome op, besides being a fashion plate and a social butterfly and the heir to millions. His idea is we ought to keep you as a sort of show piece, and not let you—"

"Go to hell!" Jack said, all red in the face.

"But I persuaded him to let me take the cotton packing off you tonight," I continued. "So meet me at Van Ness and Geary before eleven o'clock."

"Action?" He was all eagerness.

"Maybe."

"What are we going to do?"

"Bring your little pop-gun along." An idea came into my head and I worded it. "You'd better be all dressed up—evening duds."

"Dinner coat?"

"No, the limit—everything but the high hat. Now for your behavior: you're not supposed to be an op. I'm not sure just what you're supposed to be, but it doesn't make any difference. Tom-Tom Carey will be along. You act as if you were neither my friend nor his—as if you didn't trust either of us. We'll be cagey with you. If anything is asked that you don't know the answer to—you fall back on hostility. But don't crowd Carey too far. Got it?"

"I—I think so." He spoke slowly, screwing up his forehead. "I'm to act as if I was going along on the same business as you, but that outside of that we weren't

lights. In the road that was half moon-silver, half shadow-gray, the machine barely crept along for perhaps a mile. We stopped in the shade of tall shrubs that darkened a spot of the road.

"All ashore that's going ashore," Tom-Tom Carey said, and got out of the car.

Jack and I followed him. Carey took off his overcoat and threw it into the machine.

"The place is just around the bend, back from the road," he told us. "Damn this moon! I was counting on fog."

I said nothing, nor did Jack. The boy's face was white and excited.

"We'll beeline it," Carey said, leading the way across the road to a high wire fence.

He went over the fence first, then Jack, then—the sound of someone coming along the road from ahead stopped me. Signaling silence to the two men on the other side of the fence, I made myself small beside a bush. The coming steps were light, quick, feminine.

A girl came into the moonlight just ahead. She was a girl of twenty-something, neither tall nor short, thin nor plump. She was short-skirted, bare-haired, sweatered. Terror was in her white face, in the carriage of her hurrying figure, but something else was there too—more beauty than a middle-aged sleuth was used to seeing.

When she saw Carey's automobile bulking in the shadow, she stopped abruptly, with a gasp that was almost a cry.

I walked forward, saying:

"Hello, Nancy Regan."

This time the gasp was a cry.

"Oh! Oh!"

Then, unless the moonlight was playing tricks, she recognized me and terror began to go away from her. She put both hands out to me, with relief in the gesture.

"Well?" A bearish grumble came from the big boulder of a man who had appeared out of the darkness behind her. "What's all this?"

"Hello, Andy," I greeted the boulder.

"Hullo," MacElroy echoed and stood still.

Andy always did what he was told to do. He had been told to take care of Miss Newhall. I looked at the girl and then at him again.

"Is this Miss Newhall?" I asked.

"Yeah," he rumbled. "I came down like you said, but she told me she didn't want me—wouldn't let me in the house. But you hadn't said anything about coming back. So I just camped outside, moseying around, keeping my eyes on things. And when I seen her shinnying out a window a little while ago, I just went on along behind her to take care of her, like you said I was to do."

Tom-Tom Carey and Jack Counihan came back into the road, crossed it to us. The swarthy man had an automatic in one hand.

The girl's eyes were glued on mine. She paid no attention to the others.

"What is it all about?" I asked her.

"I don't know," she babbled, her hands holding on to mine, her face close to mine. "Yes, I'm Ann Newhall. I didn't know. I thought it was fun. And then when I found out it wasn't, I couldn't get out of it."

Tom-Tom Carey grunted and stirred impatiently. Jack Counihan was staring down the road. Andy MacElroy stood stolid in the road, waiting to be told what to do next. The girl never once looked from me to any of these others.

"How did you get in with them?" I demanded. "Talk fast."

Chapter Nine

Up to Her Neck

I had told the girl to talk fast. She did. For twenty minutes she stood there and turned out words in a chattering stream that had no breaks except where I cut in to keep her from straying from the path I wanted her to follow. It was jumbled, almost incoherent in spots, and not always plausible, but the notion stayed with me throughout that she was trying to tell the truth—most of the time.

And not for a fraction of a second did she turn her gaze from my eyes. It was as if she was afraid to look anywhere else.

This millionaire's daughter had, two months before, been one of a party of four young people returning late at night from some sort of social affair down the coast. Somebody suggested that they stop at a roadhouse along their way—a particularly tough joint. Its toughness was its attraction, of course—toughness was more or less of a novelty to them. They got a first-hand view of it that night, for, nobody knew just how, they found themselves taking part in a row before they had been ten minutes in the dump.

The girl's escort had shamed her by showing an unreasonable amount of cowardice. He had let Red O'Leary turn him over his knee and spank him—and had done nothing about it afterward. The other youth in the party had been not much braver. The girl, insulted by this meekness, had walked across to the red-haired giant who had wrecked her escort, and she had spoken to him loud enough for everybody to hear:

"Will you please take me home?"

Red O'Leary was glad to do it. She left him a block or two from her city house. She told him her name was Nancy Regan. He probably doubted it, but he never asked her any questions, pried into her affairs. In spite of the difference in their worlds, a genuine companionship had grown up between them. She liked him. He was so gloriously a roughneck that she saw him as a romantic figure. He was in love with her, knew she was miles above him, and so she had no trouble making him behave so far as she was concerned.

They met often. He took her to all the rowdy holes in the bay district, introduced her to yeggs, gunmen, swindlers, told her wild tales of criminal adventuring. She knew he was a crook, knew he was tied up in the Seaman's National and Golden Gate Trust jobs when they broke.

But she saw it all as a sort of theatrical spectacle. She didn't see it as it was.

She woke up the night they were in Larrouy's and were jumped by the crooks that Red had helped Papadopoulos and the others double-cross. But it was too late then for her to wriggle clear. She was blown along with Red to Papadopoulos's hangout after I had shot the big lad. She saw then what her romantic figures really were —what she had mixed herself with.

When Papadopoulos escaped, taking her with him, she was wide awake, cured, through forever with her dangerous trifling with outlaws. So she thought. She thought Papadopoulos was the little, scary old man he seemed to be—Flora's slave, a harmless old duffer too near the grave to have any evil in him. He had been whining and terrified. He begged her not to forsake him, pleaded with her while tears ran down his withered cheeks, begging her to hide him from Flora.

She took him to her country house and let him fool around in the garden, safe from prying eyes. She had no idea that he had known who she was all along, had guided her into suggesting this arrangement.

Even when the newspapers said he had been the commander-in-chief of the thug army, when the hundred-and-six thousand-dollar reward was offered for his arrest, she believed in his innocence. He convinced her that Flora and Red had simply put the blame for the whole thing on him so they could get off with lighter sentences. He was such a frightened old gink—who wouldn't have believed him?

Then her father's death in Mexico had come and grief had occupied her mind to the exclusion of most other things until this day, when Big Flora and another girl—probably Angel Grace Cardigan—had come to the house. She had been deathly afraid of Big Flora when she had seen her before. She was more afraid now.

And she soon learned that Papadopoulos was not Flora's slave but her master. She saw the old buzzard as he really was. But that wasn't the end of her awakening.

Angel Grace had suddenly tried to kill Papadopoulos. Flora had overpowered her. Grace, defiant, had told them she was Paddy's girl. Then she had screamed at Ann Newhall:

"And you, you damned fool, don't you know they killed your father? Don't you know—?"

Big Flora's fingers, around Angel Grace's throat, stopped her words. Flora tied up the Angel and turned to the Newhall girl.

"You're in it," she said brusquely. "You're in it up to your neck. You'll play along with us, or else—Here's how it stands, dearie. The old man and I are both due to step off if we're caught. And you'll do the dance with us. I'll see to that. Do what you're told, and we'll all come through all right. Get funny, and I'll beat holy hell out of you."

The girl didn't remember much after that. She had a dim recollection of going to the door and telling Andy she didn't want his services. She did this mechanically, not even needing to be prompted by the big blond woman who stood close behind her. Later, in the same fearful daze, she had gone out her bedroom window, down the vine-covered side of the porch, and away from the house, running along the road, not going anywhere, just escaping.

That was what I learned from the girl. She didn't tell me all of it. She told me very little of it in those words. But that is the story I got by combining her words, her manner of telling them, her facial expressions, with what I already knew, and what I could guess.

And not once while she talked had her eyes turned from mine. Not once had she shown that she knew there were other men standing in the road with us. She stared into my face with a desperate fixity, as if she was afraid not to, and her hands held mine as if she might sink through the ground if she let go.

"How about your servants?" I asked.

"There aren't any there now."

"Papadopoulos persuaded you to get rid of them?"

"Yes—several days ago."

"Then Papadopoulos, Flora and Angel Grace are alone in the house now?"

"Yes."

"They know you ducked?"

"I don't know. I don't think they do. I had been in my room some time. I don't think they suspected I'd dare do anything but what they told me."

It annoyed me to find I was staring into the girl's eyes as fixedly as she into mine, and that when I wanted to take my gaze away it wasn't easily done. I jerked my eyes away from her, took my hands away.

"The rest of it you can tell me later," I growled, and turned to give Andy MacElroy his orders. "You stay here with Miss Newhall until we get back from the house. Make yourselves comfortable in the car."

The girl put a hand on my arm.

"Am I—? Are you—?"

"We're going to turn you over to the police, yes," I assured her.

"No! No!"

"Don't be childish," I begged. "You can't run around with a mob of cutthroats, get yourself tied up in a flock of crimes, and then when you're tripped say, 'Excuse it, please,' and go free. If you tell the whole story in court—

including the parts you haven't told me—the chances are you'll get off. But there's no way in God's world for you to escape arrest. Come on," I told Jack and Tom-Tom Carey. "We've got to shake it up if we want to find our folks at home."

Looking back as I climbed the fence, I saw that Andy had put the girl in the car and was getting in himself.

"Just a moment," I called to Jack and Carey, who were already starting across the field.

"Thought of something else to kill time," the swarthy man complained.

I went back across the road to the car and spoke quickly and softly to Andy:

"Dick Foley and Mickey Linehan should be hanging around the neighborhood. As soon as we're out of sight, hunt 'em up. Turn Miss Newhall over to Dick. Tell him to take her with him and beat it for a phone—rouse the sheriff. Tell Dick he's to turn the girl over to the sheriff, to hold for the San Francisco police. Tell him he's not to give her up to anybody else—not even to me. Got it?"

"Got it."

"All right. After you've told him that and have given him the girl, then you bring Mickey Linehan to the Newhall house as fast as you can make it. We'll likely need all the help we can get as soon as we can get it."

"Got you," Andy said.

Chapter Ten

A Rabbit and a Lioness

"What are you up to?" Tom-Tom Carey asked suspiciously when I rejoined Jack and him.

"Detective business."

"I ought to have come down and turned the trick all by myself," he grumbled. "You haven't done a damned thing but waste time since we started."

"I'm not the one that's wasting it now."

He snorted and set out across the field again, Jack and I following him. At the end of the field there was another fence to be climbed. Then we came over a little wooded ridge and the Newhall house lay before us—a large white house, glistening in the moonlight, with yellow rectangles where blinds were down over the windows of lighted rooms.

The lighted rooms were on the ground floor. The upper floor was dark. Everything was quiet.

"Damn the moonlight!" Tom-Tom Carey repeated, bringing another automatic out of his clothes, so that he now had one in each hand.

Jack started to take his gun out, looked at me, saw I was letting mine rest, let his slide back in his pocket.

Tom-Tom Carey's face was a dark stone mask—slits for eyes, slit for mouth—the grim mask of a manhunter, a mankiller. He was breathing softly, his big chest moving gently. Beside him, Jack Counihan looked like an excited schoolboy. His face was ghastly, his eyes all stretched out of shape, and he was breathing like a tire-pump. But his grin was genuine, for all the nervousness in it.

"We'll cross to the house on this side," I whispered. "Then one of us can take the front, one the back, and the other can wait till he sees where he's needed most. Right?"

"Right," the swarthy one agreed.

"Wait!" Jack exclaimed. "The girl came down the vines from an upper window. What's the matter with my going up that way? I'm lighter than either of you. If they haven't missed her, the window would still be open. Give me ten minutes to find the window, get through it, and get myself placed. Then when you attack I'll be there behind them. How's that?" he demanded applause.

"And what if they grab you as soon as you light?" I objected.

"Suppose they do. I can make enough racket for you

to hear. You can gallop to the attack while they're busy with me. That'll be just as good."

"Blue hell!" Tom-Tom Carey barked. "What good's all that? The other way's best. One of us at the front door, one at the back, kick 'em in and go in shooting."

"If this new one works, it'll be better," I gave my opinion. "If you want to jump in the furnace, Jack, I won't stop you. I won't cheat you out of your heroics."

"No!" the swarthy man snarled. "Nothing doing!"

"Yes," I contradicted him. "We'll try it. Better take twenty minutes, Jack. That won't give you any time to waste."

He looked at his watch and I at mine, and he turned toward the house.

Tom-Tom Carey, scowling darkly, stood in his way. I cursed and got between the swarthy man and the boy. Jack went around my back and hurried away across the too-bright space between us and the house.

"Keep your feet on the ground," I told Carey. "There are a lot of things to this game you don't know anything about."

"Too damned many!" he snarled, but he let the boy go.

There was no open second-story window on our side of the building. Jack rounded the rear of the house and went out of sight.

A faint rustling sounded behind us. Carey and I spun together. His guns went up. I stretched out an arm across them, pushing them down.

"Don't have a hemorrhage," I cautioned him. "This is just another of the things you don't know about."

The rustling had stopped.

"All right," I called softly.

Mickey Linehan and Andy MacElroy came out of the tree-shadows.

Tom-Tom Carey stuck his face so close to mine that I'd have been scratched if he had forgotten to shave that day.

"You double-crossing—"

"Behave! Behave! A man of your age!" I admonished him. "None of these boys want any of your blood money."

"I don't like this gang stuff," he snarled. "We—"

"We're going to need all the help we can get," I interrupted, looking at my watch. I told the two operatives:

"We're going to close in on the house now. Four of us ought to be able to wrap it up snug. You know Papadopoulos, Big Flora and Angel Grace by description. They're in there. Don't take any chances with them—Flora and Papadopoulos are dynamite. Jack Counihan is trying to ease inside now. You two look after the back of the joint. Carey and I will take the front. We'll make the play. You see that nobody leaks out on us. Forward march!"

The swarthy man and I headed for the front porch—a wide porch, grown over with vines on the side, yellowly illuminated now by the light that came through four curtained French windows.

We hadn't taken our first steps across the porch when one of these tall windows moved—opened.

The first thing I saw was Jack Counihan's back.

He was pushing the casement open with a hand and foot, not turning his head.

Beyond the boy—facing him across the brightly lighted room—stood a man and a woman. The man was old, small, scrawny, wrinkled, pitifully frightened—Papadopoulos. I saw he had shaved off his straggly white mustache. The woman was tall, full-bodied, pink-fleshed and yellow-haired—a she-athlete of forty, with clear gray eyes set deep in a handsome brutal face—Big Flora Brace. They stood very still, side by side, watching the muzzle of Jack Counihan's gun.

While I stood in front of the window looking at this scene, Tom-Tom Carey, his two guns up, stepped past me, going through the tall window to the boy's side. I did not follow him into the room.

Papadopoulos's scary brown eyes darted to the swarthy man's face. Flora's gray ones moved there deliberately, and then looked past him to me.

"Hold it, everybody!" I ordered, and moved away from the window, to the side of the porch where the vines were thinnest.

Leaning out between the vines, so my face was clear in the moonlight, I looked down the side of the building. A shadow in the shadow of the garage could have been a man. I put an arm out in the moonlight and beckoned. The shadow came toward me—Mickey Linehan. Andy MacElroy's head peeped around the back of the house. I beckoned again and he followed Mickey.

I returned to the open window.

Papadopoulos and Flora—a rabbit and a lioness—stood looking at the guns of Carey and Jack. They looked again at me when I appeared, and a smile began to curve the woman's full lips.

Mickey and Andy came up and stood beside me. The woman's smile died grimly.

"Carey," I said, "you and Jack stay as is. Mickey, Andy, go in and take hold of our gifts from God."

When the two operatives stepped through the window —things happened.

Papadopoulos screamed.

Big Flora lunged against him, knocking him at the back door.

"Go! Go!" she roared.

Stumbling, staggering, he scrambled across the room.

Flora had a pair of guns—sprung suddenly into her hands. Her big body seemed to fill the room, as if by willpower she had become a giantess. She charged—straight at the guns Jack and Carey held—blotting the back door and the fleeing man from their fire.

A blur to one side was Andy MacElroy moving.

I had a hand on Jack's gun-arm.

"Don't shoot," I muttered in his ear.

Flora's guns thundered together. But she was tumbling. Andy had crashed into her. Had thrown himself at her legs as a man would throw a boulder.

When Flora tumbled, Tom-Tom Carey stopped waiting.

His first bullet was sent so close past her that it clipped her curled yellow hair. But it went past—caught Papadopoulos just as he went through the door. The bullet took him low in the back—smeared him out on the floor.

Carey fired again—again—again—into the prone body.

"It's no use," I growled. "You can't make him any deader."

He chuckled and lowered his guns.

"Four into a hundred and six." All his ill-humor, his grimness was gone. "That's twenty-six thousand, five hundred dollars each of those slugs was worth to me."

Andy and Mickey had wrestled Flora into submission and were hauling her up off the floor.

I looked from them back to the swarthy man, muttering, "It's not all over yet."

"No?" He seemed surprised. "What next?"

"Stay awake and let your conscience guide you," I replied, and turned to the Counihan youngster. "Come along, Jack."

I led the way out through the window and across the porch, where I leaned against the railing. Jack followed and stood in front of me, his gun still in his hand, his face white and tired from nervous tension. Looking over his shoulder, I could see the room we had just quit. Andy and Mickey, and Flora sitting between them on a sofa. Carey stood a little to one side, looking curiously at Jack and me.

We were in the middle of the band of light that came through the open window. We could see inside—except that Jack's back was that way—and could be seen from there, but our talk couldn't be overheard unless we made it loud.

All that was as I wanted it.

"Now tell me about it," I ordered Jack.

Chapter Eleven

JACK'S STORY

"WELL, I found the open window," the boy began.

"I know all that part," I cut in. "You came in and told your friends—Papadopoulos and Flora—about the girl's escape, and that Carey and I were coming. You advised them to make out you had captured them single-handed. That would draw Carey and me in. With you unsuspected behind us, it would be easy for the three of you to grab the two of us. After that you could stroll down the road and tell Andy I had sent you for the girl. That was a good scheme—except that you didn't know I had Dick and Mickey up my sleeve, didn't know I wouldn't let you get behind me. But all that isn't what I want to know. I want to know why you sold us out—and what you think you're going to do now."

"Are you crazy?" His young face was bewildered, his young eyes horrified. "Or is this some—?"

"Sure, I'm crazy," I confessed. "Wasn't I crazy enough to let you lead me into that trap in Sausalito? But I wasn't too crazy to figure it out afterward. I wasn't too crazy to see that Ann Newhall was afraid to look at you. I'm not crazy enough to think you could have captured Papadopoulos and Flora unless they wanted you to. I'm crazy—but in moderation."

Jack laughed—a reckless young laugh, but too shrill. His eyes didn't laugh with mouth and voice. While he was laughing his eyes looked from me to the gun in his hand and back to me.

"Talk, Jack," I pleaded huskily, putting a hand on his shoulder. "For God's sake why did you do it?"

The boy shut his eyes, gulped, and his shoulders twitched. When his eyes opened they were hard and glittering and full of merry hell.

"The worst part of it," he said harshly, moving his shoulder from under my hand, "is that I wasn't a very good crook, was I? I didn't succeed in deluding you."

I said nothing.

"I suppose you've earned your right to the story," he went on after a little pause. His voice was consciously monotonous, as if he was deliberately keeping out of it every tone or accent that might seem to express emotion. He was too young to talk naturally. "I met Ann Newhall three weeks ago, in my own home. She had gone to school with my sisters, though I had never met her before. We knew each other at once, of course—I knew she was Nancy Regan, she knew I was a Continental operative.

"So we went off by ourselves and talked things over. Then she took me to see Papadopoulos. I liked the old boy and he liked me. He showed me how we together could accumulate unheard-of piles of wealth. So there you are. The prospect of all that money completely devastated my morals. I told him about Carey as soon as I had heard from you, and I led you into that trap, as you say. He thought it would be better if you stopped bothering us before you found the connection between Newhall and Papadopoulos.

"After that failure, he wanted me to try again, but I refused to have a hand in any more fiascos. There's nothing sillier than a murder that doesn't come off. Ann Newhall is quite innocent of everything except folly. I don't think she has the slightest suspicion that I have had any part in the dirty work beyond refraining from having everybody arrested. That, my dear Sherlock, about concludes the confession."

I had listened to the boy's story with a great show of sympathetic attentiveness. Now I scowled at him and spoke accusingly, but still not without friendliness.

"Stop spoofing! The money Papadopoulos showed you didn't buy you. You met the girl and were too soft to turn her in. But your vanity—your pride in looking at yourself as a pretty cold proposition—wouldn't let you admit it even to yourself. You had to have a hard-boiled front. So you were meat to Papadopoulos's grinder. He gave you a part you could play to yourself—a super-gentleman-crook, a master-mind, a desperate suave villain, and all that kind of romantic garbage. That's the way you went, my son. You went as far as possible beyond what was needed to save the girl from the hoosegow—just to show the world, but chiefly yourself, that you were not acting through sentimentality, but according to your own reckless desires. There you are. Look at yourself."

Whatever he saw in himself—what I had seen or something else—his face slowly reddened, and he wouldn't look at me. He looked past me at the distant road.

I looked into the lighted room beyond him. Tom-Tom Carey had advanced to the center of the floor, where he stood watching us. I jerked a corner of my mouth at him—a warning.

"Well," the boy began again, but he didn't know what to say after that. He shuffled his feet and kept his eyes from my face.

I stood up straight and got rid of the last trace of my hypocritical sympathy.

"Give me your gun, you lousy rat!" I snarled at him.

He jumped back as if I had hit him. Craziness writhed

in his face. He jerked his gun chest-high.

Tom-Tom Carey saw the gun go up. The swarthy man fired twice. Jack Counihan was dead at my feet.

Mickey Linehan fired once. Carey was down on the floor, bleeding from the temple.

I stepped over Jack's body, went into the room, knelt beside the swarthy man. He squirmed, tried to say something, died before he could get it out. I waited until my face was straight before I stood up.

Big Flora was studying me with narrowed gray eyes. I stared back at her.

"I don't get it all yet," she said slowly, "but if you—"

"Where's Angel Grace?" I interrupted.

"Tied to the kitchen table," she informed me, and went on with her thinking aloud. "You've dealt a hand that—"

"Yeah," I said sourly, "I'm another Papadopoulos."

Her big body suddenly quivered. Pain clouded her handsome brutal face. Two tears came out of her lower eyelids.

I'm damned if she hadn't loved the old scoundrel!

Chapter Twelve

The Benefit of the Breaks

It was after eight in the morning when I got back to the city. I ate breakfast and then went up to the Agency, where I found the Old Man going through his morning mail.

"It's all over," I told him. "Papadopoulos knew Nancy Regan was Taylor Newhall's heiress. When he needed a hiding-place after the bank jobs flopped, he got her to take him down to the Newhall country place. He had two holds on her. She pitied him as a misused old duffer, and she was—even if innocently—an accomplice after the fact in the stick-ups.

"Pretty soon Papa Newhall had to go to Mexico on business. Papadopoulos saw a chance to make something. If Newhall was knocked off, the girl would have millions—and the old thief knew he could take them away from her. He sent Barrows down to the border to buy the murder from some Mexican bandits. Barrows put it over, but talked too much. He told a girl in Nogales that he had to go back 'to 'Frisco to collect plenty from an old Greek,' and then he'd return and buy her the world. The girl passed the news on to Tom-Tom Carey. Carey put a lot of twos together and got at least a dozen for an answer. He followed Barrows up here.

"Angel Grace was with him the morning he called on Barrows here—to find out if his 'old Greek' really was Papadopoulos, and where he could be found. Barrows was too full of morphine to listen to reason. He was so dope-deadened that even after the dark man began to reason with a knife-blade he had to whittle Barrows all up before he began to feel hurt. The carving sickened Angel Grace. She left, after vainly trying to stop Carey. And when she read in the afternoon papers what a finished job he had made of it, she tried to commit suicide, to stop the images from crawling around in her head.

"Carey got all the information Barrows had, but Barrows didn't know where Papadopoulos was hiding. Papadopoulos learned of Carey's arrival—you know how he learned. He sent Arlie to stop Carey. Carey wouldn't give the barber a chance—until the swarthy man began to suspect Papadopoulos might be at the Newhall place. He drove down there, letting Arlie follow. As soon as Arlie discovered his destination, Arlie closed in, hell-bent on stopping Carey at any cost. That was what Carey wanted. He gunned Arlie, came back to town, got hold of me, and took me down to help wind things up.

"Meanwhile, Angel Grace, in the cooler, had made friends with Big Flora. She knew Flora but Flora didn't know her. Papadopoulos had arranged a crush-out for Flora. It's always easier for two to escape than one. Flora took the Angel along, took her to Papadopoulos. The Angel went for him, but Flora knocked her for a loop.

"Flora, Angel Grace and Ann Newhall, alias Nancy Regan, are in the county jail," I wound up. "Papadopoulos, Tom-Tom Carey and Jack Counihan are dead."

I stopped talking and lighted a cigarette, taking my time, watching cigarette and match carefully throughout the operation. The Old Man picked up a letter, put it down without reading it, picked up another.

"They were killed in course of making the arrests?" His mild voice held nothing but its usual unfathomable politeness.

"Yes. Carey killed Papadopoulos. A little later he shot Jack. Mickey—not knowing—not knowing anything except that the dark man was shooting at Jack and me —we were standing apart talking—shot and killed Carey." The words twisted around my tongue, wouldn't come out straight. "Neither Mickey nor Andy know that Jack— Nobody but you and I know exactly what the thing—exactly what Jack was doing. Flora Brace and Ann Newhall did know, but if we say he was acting on orders all the time, nobody can deny it."

The Old Man nodded his grandfatherly face and smiled, but for the first time in the years I had known him I knew what he was thinking. He was thinking that if Jack had come through alive we would have had the nasty choice between letting him go free or giving the Agency a black eye by advertising the fact that one of our operatives was a crook.

I threw away my cigarette and stood up. The Old Man stood also, and held out a hand to me.

"Thank you," he said.

I took his hand, and I understood him, but I didn't have anything I wanted to confess—even by silence.

"It happened that way," I said deliberately. "I played the cards so we would get the benefit of the breaks—but it just happened that way."

He nodded, smiling benignantly.

"I'm going to take a couple of weeks off," I said from the door.

I felt tired, washed out.